Acapulco Nights

K. J. GILLENWATER

ISBN: 1516975707
ISBN-13: 978-1516975709

Cover art design by K. J. Gillenwater
Photograph by Everything/Shutterstock

First print publication: September 2015

Chapter One

Joaquin Hernandez de León. A name I hadn't thought about in more than ten years. Finding my husband on the Internet stunned me for a moment. I couldn't breathe.

The soft yellow walls of my home office disappeared, and my gaze narrowed at the web page in front of me.

Joaquin.

"Hey, Suzie! Are you almost ready to go?"

In a flash, I hit the print key on my computer and minimized my Internet browser window.

"You're going to miss your plane." James, my fiancé, stood in the doorway.

I sat with my back to him, trying to regain my composure. I felt the heat in my cheeks and knew if I turned to look at him, he would know something was up.

I fussed with a stack of papers next to my computer. "I'm almost ready to go. Sorry it took me so long to find what I needed." I spun around in my chair.

James had that cute little frown on his face I loved. He looked aggravated and adorable all at the same time.

I smiled. "Why don't I grab what I need here, and you start

1

warming up the car in the garage?" Seeing the printed pages waiting in the tray of my printer, I itched to pick them up and read them.

"We need to get going. It takes a lot longer to get through security nowadays, remember?" He looked at me expectantly.

As casually as I could, I switched off my computer and then swept the newly printed papers out of the tray. "Just some ideas for places to see while Janice and I are in Acapulco."

I folded them up and jammed them into the pocket of my carry-on. As I zippered my bag closed, my stomach dropped at the deceit.

*

"Could you put up your tray table please, miss?" The flight attendant stood right next to my seat.

"Oh, I'm sorry." I had been daydreaming. James had been on my mind and the uncertain look on his face as he shipped me off at the airport in San Antonio. I wondered what my fiancé was thinking right now as he drove to his conference in Dallas. It would be reassuring to have him in the seat next to me before the nerves set in again.

"Well, we can't have this tray table down, if you want to land." She gave me the perky smile that apparently had been issued with every uniform on this airline.

I grabbed the book off my tray I was supposed to be reading, and the flight attendant whisked away my empty drink cup and a crumpled bag of peanuts.

"Is there any way I could get one more beer?" I wished I could go back to San Antonio and pretend none of this was real.

She looked down her nose. "Two's the limit on any flight. Sorry. You'll have to wait until you get there."

The one time I wanted to drink myself into oblivion, I couldn't. Served me right. I was weak. Drinking wouldn't change anything anyway. The plane would land in Acapulco in a few minutes, and I didn't want to leave my seat. It would be so much nicer to stay here in this uncomfortable, narrow seat with the too-smiley flight attendant for companionship. That would be okay. Really.

I wasn't much of a drinker, but along with the standard airplane pretzels, a couple of beers seemed reasonable to take the edge off. Instead, the alcohol had twisted my stomach in knots.

Maybe it had been a good thing Ms. Perky Flight Attendant wouldn't let me have another. I'd never been interested in finding out if those air sickness bags did the job or not.

Janice would be waiting for me in Acapulco. I had to buck up, shake off those nerves, and be ready to play the good friend. I didn't need her to be questioning my state of mind.

Her flight from Chicago arrived an hour before mine. I could see her in my mind's eye: her gawky figure draped in clothes two sizes too big. She liked things loose on her body. I tried to convince her for years she should show off her athletic shape once in awhile. She had zero self-confidence about her appearance.

How she would manage to hide her body in a bathing suit was anybody's guess. I would bet a dollar, however, that Janice would figure out a way to do it.

The airplane pulled up to the gate. I slid out of my seat and grabbed my carry-on from the bin over my head. The papers with Joaquin on them were tucked safely inside.

My body anticipated the fresh air, but I forgot we were in Acapulco. Steamy, tropical Acapulco. Instead of a refreshing waft of crisp air, a warm mist enveloped me like an unwanted embrace.

Memories from my last trip to Acapulco came flooding back, but I pushed them into the darkest corner of my mind. I had been a different person then. Sometimes I ached for that old me.

*

"Suzie!"

The excited pitch of Janice's voice rose above the cacophony in the airport as I made my way from Customs. I scanned the throngs of people and instantly recognized her long, thin face. She had a much shorter haircut than I remembered, but it flattered her.

"Janice!" I pushed my way through the crowd to reach her, pulling my heavy suitcase.

Janice took my carry-on from my shoulder. "Can you believe this place?" She indicated the morass of people and luggage jammed in the airport. "How insane is this?"

Her smile was infectious. My mood lightened just by being in her presence.

"Crazy," I said with as much enthusiasm as I could muster. This trip filled me with a certain amount of dread and nervousness, but I did my best to put on a happy face.

She stopped and looked at me, "Duh! Come here, give me a hug!" She wrapped her free arm around my shoulders.

I stood there, both hands yanking on my stubborn suitcase. I had over-packed—the wheels that were supposed to speed me along through the airport weren't even touching the ground. The bulging middle of my suitcase dragged, undignified, on the tile floor.

I gave up the fight against too many pairs of shoes stuffed in the bottom of my bag and gave my old friend a half-hug.

"And how have you been?" Janice had a nervous kind of energy. An energy that, unless she used it regularly, could turn easily into agitation.

"I've been doing all right," I answered through gritted teeth. I hoped the wheels on my suitcase would somehow make themselves useful. Even leaning all my weight forward, the suitcase stubbornly dragged on the ground.

She led me right out the automatic sliding doors to a taxi stand. I let go of my suitcase and tipped it up into its at-rest position.

Definitely need to rearrange the shoes for the trip home.

Janice giggled. "You have no idea how much fun we are going to have! The hotel I picked has all sorts of activities and events." She squeezed my arm while she waved down a taxi. "I'm so glad you decided to come along after all. It wouldn't have been the same without you."

"Well, it was nice to be invited. Not often that I get the chance to do some girlfriend bonding."

"It's been too long, hasn't it?"

"Yeah, that's for sure." I couldn't remember the last time Janice and I had gotten together for more than a quick weekend visit. Over the years our lives had grown more distant, especially once I'd move to Texas. "So, since I know you so well, what activity did you sign me up for?"

"Why, I didn't sign you up for anything." Then, she rushed right into it. "But there was one thing I knew you would love, and if I didn't put our names down ahead of time, I thought we might not get a spot."

A taxi pulled up to the curb, and the driver popped the trunk. He got out of the car, took my overstuffed bag from my hands, and lifted it into the back.

"When were you planning on telling me? Or were you going to spring it on me at the most inappropriate time?"

My sarcasm lost on her, she gushed, "We're going kayaking!"

Our driver waited for us, holding open the passenger door. I slid in, wondering what made Janice think I would enjoy paddling a small boat with a tendency to flip over. I wasn't out-of-shape, but a few rounds of tennis would've been more my style.

Janice spoke to the driver, most likely giving him the name of our hotel. I held back my question.

Janice slid into the seat next to me.

"Kayaking?"

"I signed us up for all three levels." Janice squeezed my arm. "By the end of our trip, we should be experts." Her long, thin legs didn't fit in a car this size. Her knees squished up against the front seat, but she didn't seem to care about her discomfort. All of her mental energy focused on our Acapulco adventure.

"All three levels, huh?" What more could there be to learn beyond some paddling? Maybe I could find a way to skip out on lessons two and three. Feign illness? Heat stroke? A debilitating sunburn?

"I wanted to sign us up for the trapeze class, but—"

"Trapeze class?"

"I know!" Janice continued blithely, "That had been my first choice, too, but they've been closed down for two weeks due to some safety issues."

I was glad she didn't elaborate on what the safety issues were nor how they figured out a problem existed with safety in the first place. Kayaking would be just fine.

"Is it a group class?" I imagined making a fool out of myself, dropping my paddle in the water, flipping over repeatedly, wearing those silly looking helmets. In front of Janice, I couldn't care less, but in front of strangers—

"I think so," Janice answered without noticing the trepidation in my voice. "Wait until you see the hotel, Suzie. We have a suite with this huge living area. And a whirlpool bath! Oh, and an ocean view!"

She gave me the details of our accommodations as we drove through the outskirts of town. Dozens of tarpaper shacks and tarp tents lined up along the dusty roads, blocked off from traffic by broken chain link fencing. Some of the squatters' homes bore hand-painted signs saying *propiedad privada*— private property. A handful of dirty-looking children, dressed in clothes much too hot for such a climate, played soccer with a half-deflated soccer ball, aiming for goals made from cardboard taped together.

Mexico hadn't changed much in the last decade.

"So how's James? How's life in San Antonio?" Janice asked brightly.

"Good." I hoped that Janice wouldn't take the questioning

any further than that. Question answered. No further details needed.

"That's all I get from you, 'good'?"

Dang it. Guess Janice had to have more than a one word answer. "James and I are living in the same house, have the same jobs." There, that should satisfy her.

"And haven't picked a wedding date?"

The one question I'd dreaded. "Oh, Janice, don't you give me a hard time, too."

"How can I not? You've been engaged for four years, Suze. People are starting to wonder."

"People? What people?"

"Okay, so your mom and I have been wondering. What's going on with you two? Is it cold feet or something else?"

We both gripped our respective door handles as our driver took a sharp turn at a pretty fast clip.

"You've been talking to my mom about me and James?" I should've known. My mother had turned into the Oprah of Buffalo Grove. She could pry information out of anyone.

"Who else would I be talking to, the mailman?"

"Janice, I know you and my mother are close, but—"

She waggled her finger. "Remember? You told me to keep an eye on her. We meet once a month for brunch, and your love life is our favorite topic of conversation."

"Great." I slumped back. They were like Oprah and Gayle, yukking it up over pancakes and coffee. Dishing on my relationship status.

"Hey, we care about you, dummy. I think James is a great guy and all, but if he can't commit, maybe you should be questioning his feelings for you."

"Janice, it's not James who cancelled. I did. I couldn't bear telling my mom." Or you, I thought, as concern filled her eyes.

"You cancelled? All three times? What's going on? I thought you loved James. He's so perfect for you."

"I do love him, but—" Oh, how I wished I could confide in her at that moment. But if I did, I knew I would lose her friendship, and this time it would be permanent. "It's complicated." When you can't bear to tell the truth, obfuscation was a good way to go.

Janice looked pained. My oldest and dearest friend, and I couldn't be straight with her.

Janice grabbed my hand. "When you're ready to talk, I'm here."

God, why did she have to be so loyal? So kind and so sweet? I didn't deserve it. In fact, I didn't deserve James either. I had lived with this deception for so long I didn't know how to act any differently.

I squeezed her hand. "Thanks."

As we approached the center of the city, the shacks were replaced by brightly-colored adobe walls of pink, blue, yellow, and orange. These were the more middle-class homes hidden behind decorative wrought iron gates. Bright pink bougainvillea grew everywhere in this town, and the vines dipped and looped around the intricate metalwork, softening the angles and points.

The colors became a blur as I thought about the papers in my carry-on bag. The first chance I got, I would pull out those pages I printed off the Internet and find out where Joaquin worked. Then, once I tracked him down, he and I needed to have a long talk.

My stomach dropped down to my knees at that thought. Where to start after all these years? How to explain myself? I imagined calling him on the phone and saying, "Hey, remember me, your long lost wife? Well, I'm in town, and I need a divorce." Not the best way to start a conversation with a husband I'd abandoned years ago.

Husband.

That term sounded so foreign to me. Did Joaquin and I really get married? After twelve years of wondering what had happened to him and hiding my secret from everyone, I'd managed to find him with a few clicks of my mouse. What had been impossible only a few years earlier had changed with the birth of the Internet. Search engines, online white pages, reverse telephone lookups—I no longer had an excuse. I'd told myself for years that once I found Joaquin, I'd get that divorce. Snip, snap.

Now that I had my husband's location, I knew it wouldn't be quite that easy. I couldn't take care of my problem with one casual conversation. I'd have to face Joaquin and explain myself. If I wanted to marry James, I would have to put aside my nerves and deal with the situation. I couldn't see another way.

The taxi pulled up to our hotel: an overly-grand, sprawling building that hugged the coastline. Tall, exotic palm trees lined the drive, their feathery fronds waving in the tropical breeze.

Janice did a little dance with her feet on the floor of the cab, "We're here! Can you believe it?"

I tried to match her enthusiasm, "What do you want to do first? Beach? Or maybe try out that whirlpool tub?"

As I stepped out of the taxi, I saw the massive sign out front with the name of our hotel in huge blue and yellow lettering: Playa Del Mexico.

My heart stopped for an instant. A loud ringing in my ears blocked out whatever Janice said to me.

Joaquin's hotel. The one in the Internet article. It couldn't be.

Standing there, unable to speak, I slipped my hand into my carry-on bag. I pulled out those pages. I had to see for myself.

I unfolded the now-wrinkled sheaf of papers. Joaquin's smiling face looked back at me. I scanned the first paragraph of the article.

"Hey, Suze, let's get a move on. The vacation starts inside the building, not out on the sidewalk." Janice tugged at my sleeve.

On the first printed page the name of the hotel glared at me in bold:

Playa Del Mexico.

The papers slipped from my hand like so many dry leaves. Before they hit the ground, a gust of wind swept them up and carried them away. I could chase after them, gather them up, but what would be the use? I didn't need them anymore. This was the same hotel. I knew I would find him here.

I felt it in my bones.

Chapter Two

"Are you ok?" Janice asked me for the third time.

The printed papers fluttered down the busy streets of Acapulco, lost to the wind. Here is where my journey would begin, at the Playa Del Mexico Hotel, a thousand miles from home, from James, and from the life I had built.

Somehow I found my voice, "Yes, I'm all right." Our taxi pulled away from the curb, leaving me and my suitcase behind. I dumbly reached for it.

Janice put her hand on my arm, "Let the bellboy get it. He's bringing the cart around now."

Yes, the bellboy. We were on vacation, staying at a posh hotel. No need for me to schlep my heavy suitcase.

I turned away from the street and the papers blowing away. I pasted on my widest, happiest smile. "So, what do you say we get a couple of Tequila Sunrises and get this party started?"

"Now you're talking!" Janice cheered.

Linking her arm with mine, she led me through the huge glass entrance doors at the top of a wide stone stairway.

*

"Can you believe this room?" My traveling companion plopped herself down on the suede sofa in our expansive suite. She leaned over and whipped open the mini-fridge grabbing several tiny bottles of vodka and two containers of orange juice.

I stood right inside the door. The view mesmerized me. Far below us blue water extended as far as the eye could see and beyond that a brilliant sky filled with a few puffy white clouds. I wanted to dive into that water and lose myself in its clear depths—close my eyes, hold my breath, and let the powerful tide sweep over me.

"Did you see the flyers all over the elevator?" Janice's voice brimmed with excitement.

How could I have missed dozens of bright orange flyers pasted to the inside of a gold-plated, mirrored elevator? "Yeah, the 'Welcome Fiesta'?"

"That's the one. We are so going to be there."

"You got it." I wanted to make Janice's vacation the best ever, even if I had to be willing to put up with a few dozen drunk men and several rounds of limbo in order to achieve it. "It'll be kinda funny to go to a 'welcome' party half way through our trip."

"Who cares what they name it? Guaranteed fun—and an open bar!"

I smiled as she mixed together the drinks in two of the plastic cups sitting next to the ice bucket. She seemed so relaxed and happy here. This trip would do her a world of good.

"Here," Janice handed me a cup. "We can go down to the cantina later, but it looked like you needed a drink right now. Must have been a rough week at work."

I gratefully took the cheap cup from her hand, half-filled with orange juice and vodka, and turned away from the view. Without saying a word, I took a large gulp. First beer, now vodka. I hoped I didn't get sick from the combination.

"Guess I hit the nail on the head, huh?" Janice asked with a tweak of a smile on her face.

"You could say that." I took another big swig, leaving only a trace of juice and vodka in my cup. I waited for my stomach to rebel, but it had calmed since the plane trip.

"Right back at ya." She raised her cup to me in a sort of salute, and then downed half of her drink. Giving a satisfied smack, she said dolefully, "I've had a rough *six years* at work."

"Hard to believe it's been that long."

"Straight out of law school. God, I thought I'd never pass the bar." Janice slumped back against the couch cushions, as if she were reliving the stress of the exam. "The first few months on the job were murder."

"At least you passed the first time you took it. Not everyone's that lucky." I took a seat in a comfortable-looking wingback chair.

"Yeah, I guess you're right. Before I passed it, I felt as if I had the life sucked out of me — working, studying, working, and studying some more." She took a long sip from her plastic cup. "But looking back on it, I'm not sure why I bothered."

"What do you mean? You've always wanted to be a lawyer. In fact, I can't remember you *not* talking about it. I seem to recall you were going to work for the best law firm in Chicago and make partner before you turned thirty-five."

"*Thirty*. Make partner before I turned *thirty*."

"All right, make partner before you were thirty." I waved my hand at the minor discrepancy.

"Well, maybe I had been a little ambitious."

The tired look on her face prompted me to ask, "Are you happy there?"

"Sure, I'm happy," Janice said in the most unhappy voice ever. Even the usually crazy, tousled hair on her head drooped at her words.

"Doesn't sound like it. In fact, when I saw you in the airport you looked as if you'd just escaped from prison or something. As if you haven't seen the sun in months."

"I haven't. Remember, I live in Chicago? Winter lasts

almost all year long up there."

"Ha, ha." I curled up in the oversized chair. "But you have your dream job, and you're great at it. Plus, you're making the big bucks, and that lets you do things, like invite your best friend to Mexico."

"I know, I know. But for the past year or so, I've been in this funk. I'm not quite sure what it is. First, I thought it was all the stress, so I squeezed in a psychiatrist every other month. After dumping a few thousand dollars into that, I actually started to feel worse." She took another gulp of her drink. "Then, I finally figured out what it was."

"What?"

"I wanted what everyone else had. What you and James have."

"Oh." I looked down into my cup at the dregs of my screwdriver.

"Most weekends you know where I am? In the office. And if I'm not in the office, I'm working at home." She opened up the mini-fridge again, grabbed another orange juice and started unpeeling the seal around another tiny bottle of vodka. "The only time I go outside is on the way to a business lunch with a client or when I go for a run. You know what a big weekend is for me? Renting a DVD and making microwave popcorn." She poured the orange juice and vodka into her cup, stirring it with her finger.

"Have you ever thought about finding a new job?" I held out my cup to her, and she refilled it for me. "Something at a smaller firm? Maybe moving away from the city?"

"How would that help, Suzie? I know I'd end up doing the same things: working my ass off, staying in instead of going out." She took a little sip of her drink. "Maybe I would have more free time, but you know how I would spend it? Rent two DVDs and maybe throw in a pack of M&Ms with the popcorn."

"Oh, I'm sure it's not that bad."

"Don't patronize me, Suze. Don't you think by now I know myself better than you do?" She tossed the empty vodka bottle into the trash.

"I didn't mean—"

She held up her hand. "I'm sorry, I didn't mean to bite your head off. It just gets so frustrating sometimes. It's as if I missed the dating boat and now it's too late." She kicked off her sandals and tucked her feet underneath her lanky body. "How can I make up for all that lost time? I'm totally behind the curve."

"It's never too late, Janice. Never. Look at James."

"Yes, let's look at James," she sighed.

"What do you mean by that?" I set my cup on the coffee table.

"Well, he's adorable, he's successful, he's witty, and, of course, he fell in love with you at the drop of a hat."

"Now, that's not exactly true—"

"Okay, so he fell in love with you after one date." She swirled her drink in her hand, watching the ice spiral around.

I couldn't argue with that one. James had fallen completely head-over-heels for me before I even knew what hit me. I had it pretty easy. Time to change the subject before we started dissecting my relationship again. "There are men out there for you, I promise."

"Where?" she said, exasperated. "At the gym? Tried that. At work? Tried that more times than I want to remember. In my running group? Trust me. There's no one out there for me."

"There's someone out there for everyone."

"Who says? Have they done some empirical study? I hear it all the time, but how do we know it's true? I haven't had one steady boyfriend in my entire life. In fact, I can count the number of dates I've had on one hand. *One hand*, Suzie. There *has* to be something wrong with me."

"There's nothing wrong with you."

"How do you know?"

"I just know."

"Because how, you are some expert on men and what they find attractive?" She set her drink down next to mine, plucked the Mexican equivalent of a bag of Doritos out of a basket on top of the refrigerator, and popped it open.

"No, but—"

"Let's change the subject. I'm here to relax, not freak out about my man problems." After crunching a few chips, she finished the last few drops of her drink. "That would take more than ten days to solve anyway."

Janice got up from the couch and grabbed her sandals. She placed her empty cup on the small table near the windows and went over to her bags. "I'm putting on my bathing suit, grabbing my sarong, and we are out the door." She unzipped her suitcase with a flourish.

The great thing about Acapulco is no one cared if you wore nothing more than a bathing suit to the bars, restaurants, stores, even the movie theater. And in a resort hotel like Playa Del Mexico, most of those things could be found right on site. It would probably even be acceptable to wear a bathrobe to breakfast.

As Janice dashed into the bedroom to change, I unfolded a luggage rack I found in the entryway closet, dragged my monster of a suitcase out of the corner where the bellhop left it, and tried to sling it on top of the contraption. After several unsuccessful attempts to land it onto the miniscule rack, I gave up in defeat and laid it on the tile floor. Unzipping it, I hunted for my bathing suit—a very modest two-piece.

Janice dashed back into the room, her short hair spiking up wildly from her head. "What do you think?" She modeled her beach wear for me, taking several turns, looking like Vanna White hopped up on Power Bars. Her aggravation over men, her job, and her lawyer life had disappeared for the time being.

"You look fantastic!" A riotously bright-green bikini showed off her slender figure with its barely-there curves and revealed how hard she worked to keep it that way. Her stomach was taut, her legs slim and muscular.

"Do you think so?" The body-conscious Janice had

returned, and she quickly tied a flowered, flowing sarong around her boy-like hips.

"You know you do."

Clearly wanting to stay off the topic of her bikini-clad self, she asked me, "And what are you waiting around for? Go get changed, missy! Happy Hour's probably half over by now."

"It's only two o'clock in the afternoon," I pointed out.

She focused a steady gaze on me. "Get your butt in there and change already." She tapped her finger on her waterproof watch. "This is a ten-day vacation, and half-a-day is already over."

"Yes, ma'am." I picked up my swimsuit and a pair of shorts. Janice was right, we only had ten days to spend in Acapulco.

I closed the bedroom door behind me, grateful for a few quiet moments to reflect on my plan. Ten days. Not a lot of time. I slipped off my traveling clothes and pulled on my swimming suit.

A small, leather-bound book caught my eye by the phone on the nightstand—the hotel directory. Maybe I could find a phone number for the office or even the general manager. Tomorrow I could find some time to slip away and make a few phone calls, get some questions answered about Joaquin. Maybe the Internet article I'd found had been outdated. Could be he no longer worked here. That would be my first order of business. Couldn't quite get a divorce, if I couldn't track down my husband, now, could I?

I sat down on the bed and reached for the directory.

Someone banged on the door.

"What're you doing in there? Getting ready for the Sports Illustrated Swimsuit Edition?" Janice hollered.

Before I could even peek inside the pages, I set it back on the nightstand. I would have time to look at that later. Maybe once Janice fell asleep.

Although I wanted to do nothing more than pour over the directory and see if I could find Joaquin's name inside, I dutifully finished slipping on my suit and slicking my hair back into a ponytail.

"I'm coming!" Then, a thought struck me. I should call James. If I heard his voice, maybe it would give me the courage to hunt down Joaquin and get this over with. I eyed the phone sitting on the nightstand.

*

James had been 'the one' with a capital "O" from the very first night I'd met him.

We worked for the same software company, but in different departments, so we had never crossed paths.

Late one Tuesday when I had worked overtime, my car had a flat in the parking garage. He'd stopped to help. He'd been driving through the garage, on his way home, and had seen me standing next to my car, tire iron in hand, car manual spread out on the hood of my Jetta.

He'd rescued me. He called it that anyway. To me, he had been a cute, but older man, most likely married or divorced with the standard two kids, stopping to help an idiot. I mean, who doesn't know how to change a tire?

I thought he'd pitied me.

"Um, hey, do you need some help there?" James had asked.

I'd looked up from the grease-smeared pages of my Jetta manual. He had one hand in his pocket, and in the other he held a battered leather briefcase.

"Guess my mom was right. I should have joined Triple A."

"Nah. It's not all that hard. A monkey could do it."

I gave him a look.

"Uh, well, it would be easy enough to teach a monkey–"

He dug himself a deeper hole.

"I mean, you're a smart woman. I'm sure you can–"

"It's okay." I smiled. He had been so nervous and rumpled and adorable. I couldn't let him suffer any longer. "I appreciate your help. I hate being a cliché."

He gave me a questioning look.

"You know, damsel in distress? A woman who can't change a tire? Pretty sorry in this day and age, don't you think?"

"Not really. It's a dirty job, and I can see why you wouldn't want to mess up—uh—" He'd gestured helplessly at me and my smart business attire and office hair—my term for the twisted and clipped locks on the back of my head.

I touched my hair. "What makes you think I mind getting dirty?" I smiled.

He leaned over my shoulder and grabbed the open manual off of my hood. "First, you don't need this. See this thingie?" He held up the jack I had left on the oily, dirty parking garage floor. "You put it together like this, stick it under here." He clicked the jack handle into place and slid it under the frame of the car behind the flat. "And start pumping."

I watched as he got down on that grimy floor and pumped. "My name's Suzette, by the way."

"I'm James."

He finished jacking up the car, unscrewed the lug nuts, slid the flattened tire off, and replaced it with the spare from my trunk. By the end, his hands were dirty and his suit needed a good dry-cleaning.

"Well, that's about it. You're good to go." I handed back his suit jacket, which I'd been holding for him.

"Can I at least buy you a cup of coffee or something? Or would your wife wonder?"

He wiped his hands on a Kleenex I'd grabbed out of my car, then took the jacket and hung it over his forearm. "I don't have a wife, and I think I could spare a few moments for a pretty lady, a cup of coffee, and a piece of pie."

"Pie? When did I say pie?"

"That's the going rate for a tire change after hours."

"I see." His sense of humor put a smile on my face. "Any particular kind of pie?"

"Coconut Cream."

"I think I can manage something. Why don't you follow me? Where are you parked?"

"Next level down. Wait for me at the gate."

Our conversation over coffee and pie would have carried over into the next morning, if I'd had my way. But he had been too much of a gentleman for that. Instead, after an extra large piece of pie and two cups of coffee, he'd followed me to make sure I got home safely.

James had been much different than men I usually dated. I liked the brutes, tall and muscular with a history of playing football or soccer. These men were better with actions than with words, making them fantastic lovers, but terrible boyfriends. Once the physical attraction had run its course, the relationship soon faded or I became bored.

James had a very thin and angular frame. Not an athlete by any means. His deep green eyes were what caught me at first. They were quiet, soft eyes. His intelligence and quirky humor had been a welcome change, and we discovered we enjoyed the same things: foreign films and Dickens novels, muffins and strong coffee for breakfast, a tennis game at twilight.

James called it "love-at-first-sight," which makes absolutely no sense when trying to explain it.

I knew he was older than I, but wasn't really sure how much older. He had a bit of graying at the temples, which I found sexy, but his face was unlined and youthful. Even though it bothered him, James's age hadn't been a factor for me.

"What would your mother think, you going out with someone who's almost forty?" We'd been dating for six solid months when he burst out with this question.

We sat in my driveway, the car's engine rumbling. James held my hand and squeezed it lightly, waiting for my answer. This had been weighing on his mind for some time.

"She doesn't care." I leaned over to kiss his cheek.

"You've already told her about us?" James sounded nervous, as if we were sixteen and had stayed out past our curfew.

"I told her about you the first night we met." I laughed at his apprehension. My mother and I had grown very close over the years since my dad's death; we shared almost everything with each other.

"You did?" He turned toward me, his body angled uncomfortably in the driver's seat.

"Yes, I did. And she was okay with it. Really."

"Didn't she ask why I never got married? Doesn't she wonder why I would be interested in you?"

"Are *you* wondering why you're interested in me?" I teased, knowing he felt uncomfortable with the eleven-year gap between us.

At that, he dropped the questions and reached out for me, giving me a long, deep kiss. When he pulled back, he whispered in my ear, "I *know* why I'm interested in you."

Chapter Three

"Come on, Suze, let's get a move on! We only have so many hours of sun left!" Janice yelled through the closed bedroom door.

I sat on the bed, bathing suit on and towel in my lap, staring at the phone. Even though I knew James was on the road, most likely with his cell phone off, I wanted to dial his number.

I picked up the receiver.

"Hang on, Janice. I want to make a phone call," I called out, following the instructions on the faceplate of the phone for making an international call. I didn't care if it cost me an arm and a leg to use the hotel phone. I needed to hear his voice.

"What?" Janice's muffled voice yelled back.

I heard a distant clicking on my end and then an odd, echoing ring. "Phone call!" I enunciated as loudly as I could.

Two rings. Three rings.

Hello, you have reached James Pickford's voicemail. If you would like to leave a message, please do so after the beep. Thank you.

Even listening to such a formal message, I could clearly

imagine his lips forming those words, his dimple disappearing and reappearing as he spoke. The voicemail beep jarred me out of my thoughts, and I scrambled to say something intelligible. "Hey, honey, it's me. I wanted to let you know I got here safely. We're in Room 1210 if you need to get a hold of me. I miss you!"

I placed the phone back on the cradle, hesitant to disconnect. I had the urge to dial his number again to listen to the message for a second time, but Janice cracked the door open.

"Come on!" The tip of a straw hat poked through the door opening. "I thought you said James wouldn't be in Dallas until late tonight."

"All right. I'm ready to go." I was reluctant to leave my spot on the bed by the phone.

*

We reclined on lounge chairs under a *palapa* made from palm leaves, shaded from the intense sun, sipping behemoth margaritas and lazily watching the sailboats far from shore bob up and down on the waves. It had been a relaxing afternoon on the beach, which surprised me.

The anticipation coursing through me on the plane trip ebbed away. Maybe the two margaritas I'd consumed over the last few hours were getting to me. Or maybe the fleeting thoughts I'd had about leaving well enough alone brought me close to forgetting why I'd ever come here. No one knew I had married Joaquin, not my mother, not my friends, not even the United States government. I could set a date, get married to James, and live my life.

My mind played with the fantasy while I soaked in the sun on the warm, sandy beach. How easy it would be to enjoy a vacation with my friend, rather than search for a man I would rather not encounter.

"Peso for your thoughts." Janice set her almost-empty

glass on the small table between us. She'd slathered her long, thin nose in zinc oxide and pulled her wide-brimmed straw hat down low over her eyes.

For a moment, I wanted to confess the thoughts that plagued me—keeping this secret to myself for so many years had worn me down—but I lost my nerve.

I sipped my lukewarm margarita. "When were we going to take those sea kayaking lessons?" That should be a topic to light her fire.

Janice perked up at the mention of the word 'kayak.' "Tomorrow morning at nine o'clock sharp. Won't we have so much fun? Two hours out on that gorgeous ocean—"

"Two hours?" I coughed, choking on my drink. The heat beat down with intensity, even under the shaded *palapa*. I imagined how hot it would be out on the exposed, reflective surface of Acapulco Bay. As hot as the inside of an oven, most likely.

"I know. Not enough time. But once we learn the basics, we can rent our own kayaks and be out for as long as we like." She didn't seem to notice the look of horror on my face. "Wouldn't it be cool to paddle all the way over there?" She pointed to a jutting piece of land at the most northern point of the bay, a good ten miles away and smiled widely.

I'd landed in hell, and it was called Acapulco.

Perhaps tomorrow, if I feigned complete incompetence, I would be barred from paddling anything that floated on the water. The insurance risk would be too great for the hotel to allow a klutz like me to be out on the open water. I imagined all sorts of ways to undermine the instructor until he ordered me back to shore. I didn't mind learning how to paddle a kayak, but paddling ten miles alone on the ocean would be a completely different story.

"Let's take this vacation one step at a time." I hoped to scale down her dreams to make this trip one long workout session. "There might be some other stuff we want to do."

She thought about my suggestion for a minute. "You're

right, Suze. We don't want to tie ourselves down to any one thing. We'll have to look at the hotel schedule to see what else might be going on."

I breathed a quiet sigh of relief. Although Janice was extremely motivated, especially when it came to exercise, I knew I could easily distract her with the next big idea. Thank God for a little bit of ADD.

I reclined on my lounge chair, finished off my margarita, and we both watched the sun sink lower in the sky. Looking at my watch, I noted the late hour. "Hey, Janice, we're going to have to high-tail it back upstairs, if we want to make our reservation."

She jumped up from her lounge chair, leaving half a margarita sitting on the table. Besides being an exercise fiend, she also adored eating. Considering all the running, biking, hiking, and swimming she did on a regular basis, she could probably consume five thousand calories a day and still lose weight. Sickening.

"What are we waiting for?" She tightened the knot on her sarong.

I set down my glass, grabbed my bag full of beach supplies, and took up the rear. When that girl wanted to eat, she could really get a move on.

*

Precisely five minutes before our dinner reservation, we were both freshly showered and comfortably dressed. I, in a flowered sundress with spaghetti straps, and Janice in a flirty, short one with a scoop neckline. I called it 'tourist chic.' We were obviously American with our strappy sandals, sunglasses, and digital cameras dangling from our wrists, but at least we weren't wearing oversized t-shirts and spandex shorts. Not on the first day of our vacation, anyway.

Passing through the lobby on our way to Antonio's Cafe, which claimed to serve the "Best Taquitos in Acapulco," we crossed in front of a picture display that caught my eye.

The placard read: "Playa Del Mexico Working For You." Beneath it were Polaroid pictures of various employees, their titles and names inscribed beneath. In the top row of pictures, under the heading 'General Manager,' I saw a face that made my heart race, my palms sweat, and my eyesight blur.

"*Querida*," a rumbling male voice, almost as familiar as my own, spoke softly right behind me.

I jumped.

He touched my bare shoulder with a warm hand, and a shiver ran through me.

Janice and I both turned at the same time, but she spoke the words that filled my mind. "Joaquin! Oh, my God! I can't believe it's you!" Her thin face flushed red with excitement, and she grabbed me tightly by the arm. "Isn't this a good surprise, Suzie?"

Words gathered in my mouth, but I couldn't open my lips to release them.

"Yes, isn't this a good surprise?" Joaquin said, an odd smirk on his face.

"A surprise?" I managed to say. My stomach heaved.

"When I planned the trip and searched for a hotel, I ran across this news article online, and there was Joaquin's picture, right on the screen! I thought it would be so much fun to stay here, catch up on old times." She gave him an assessing look and touched his arm, "You haven't changed a bit, Joaquin. Not one bit."

Joaquin's effect on women had not diminished even after twelve years. He was a very attractive man and in great physical shape. The only change to his face was the well-trimmed goatee, which only deepened his handsomeness. His eyes glowed, and his beautiful white teeth flashed at us both. He gave Janice a quick hug.

I grew speechless. Janice planned all of this? God, if she only knew what really happened between Joaquin and me back then, she would have made plans to visit Cancún instead. I rubbed my clammy hands on my dress.

"Hello, Joaquin. Well, isn't this a surprise." My voice came out a bit breathless. "Janice is quite the little planner, isn't she?" I felt a touch dizzy. I wished I could sit down, but I saw no empty chair in sight.

The years between us melted away. San Antonio had all been a dream, a nice, but distant dream. I was supposed to be here, standing next to this gorgeous man. My body inched closer to his, and it seemed natural when he pulled me into his body for an embrace. His chest felt hard and warm against mine. I'd forgotten why I'd come here.

Janice stepped back a half-step, looking oddly at us both. It only lasted a moment. If I didn't know her so well, I probably never would have noticed that look at all. I pulled away from Joaquin, knowing this closeness, this attraction was not right.

James waited at home for me. He trusted me. Besides, I flew all the way to Mexico to end the mistakes I'd made in my past, not jump right back into them. What was I thinking?

Moving away from Joaquin, I could sense the frown forming between his brows. Was he angry with me? Did he want to know where I'd been all these years? Why I'd never contacted him?

Then, I remembered Janice. She would keep everything civil. Joaquin managed the place. He wouldn't want to create a scene right in the very lobby of the hotel where he was employed. Yes, that must be it.

"So, we are going to dinner, yes?" Joaquin asked, his face blank of any discernible emotion.

I looked at Janice.

"He wanted to take us to dinner. Isn't that fabulous?" Janice gushed. "There's some place he was telling me about. It looks out over the water."

I found my voice, "Yes. Wonderful." I could act as if this were a casual meeting of old friends. No need to get overly emotional about ancient history between two old lovers who just happened to be married. Yes, a married couple who hadn't spent one night together as husband and wife.

This couldn't be my life. I imagined starting out dinner with polite conversation and ending with "hey, honey, I want a divorce." I managed a strained smile.

"Let me show you the real Acapulco." Joaquin gave me a cryptic look. The smile returned to his eyes, and he directed a question to Janice. "You both like seafood, yes?"

She nodded and looked at me.

"Sure," I answered.

My knees were like Jell-o, and my heart raced like a stampeding elephant. I thought about sitting next to Joaquin at a dinner table, drinking wine, sharing a meal. A few hours in a restaurant with friends.

Friends?

Oh, I was good about lying to myself. Joaquin had been much more than a friend. How would I manage to make it through dinner and keep our twelve-year marriage a secret from Janice? Would Joaquin keep the past to himself? Maybe he, too, hoped for a more private moment to discuss what happened.

"My car's waiting outside. Are you two ready to go?" He gestured toward the glass lobby doors and a car I could see waiting outside.

"More than ready," said Janice. "I'm starving. Let's get a move on!"

I nodded my head and gave a wan smile.

I should be able manage two hours of fake smiles and chatter over guacamole and *carne asada*. How hard could that be?

Chapter Four

We sat in Joaquin's convertible with the top down. The orange-red sun setting over the bay mesmerized me. Acapulco was as beautiful as ever—tall palms lined the long curve of the white sand beach, and the sky darkened into a deep navy blue with a sparkling of stars. The sweet scent of honeysuckle rode on the breeze mixing with the salty tang of sea air.

To keep the awkwardness to a minimum, I insisted Janice sit in the front seat. That spot gave her the best view. Plus, it would keep me from strangling her at keeping such a 'surprise' from me all these weeks.

"I'm taking you to one of the best restaurants in town. Let me make a call to make sure we're getting the table I asked for." Joaquin flipped open his cell phone, dialing and driving with deftness.

We skirted along the stretch of road that hugged the bay, working our way toward the northern edge—the same lip of land Janice had pointed to earlier on the beach. I would rather be paddling that distance alone in a kayak, than be riding there with Joaquin in a candy apple red convertible with leather seats.

I doubted Janice thought the same. She was radiant and

smiling, taking in the view, the breeze, and the night air. For her, Acapulco was a dream.

Joaquin spoke some rapid Spanish into his phone, and a moment later he smiled. "It's all taken care of. Best table in the house."

"Oh, Joaquin," Janice said. "You didn't have to go to so much trouble just for us."

At that moment Joaquin looked pointedly at me in his rear view mirror. "I would move heaven and earth for you ladies."

I looked away, the intensity in his hazel gaze too much to bear. What did he want from me? If he had wanted to talk, why did he insist on taking Janice and me to a fancy restaurant?

Could it be that he thinks Janice knows? He knew she and I were good friends all those years ago. She had been there when we met. My breathing became shallow, my hands cold as panic set in.

Oh, God. This can't be happening.

What have I gotten myself into? Janice will find out, Janice will tell James—my mind whirled at the thought of my secret being exposed to him. He trusted me. He loved me. James would not forgive my deception.

*

"So, I've been wanting to ask you this for awhile now," I said.

James and I sat in a movie theater, the rest of the audience filtering out into the aisle while the credits played.

"What?" He set his empty soda cup into the half-full bucket of popcorn and wiped his greasy hands on a napkin.

"Why would a fabulous guy like you still be single? Why hasn't some hot woman snatched you up?" I crumpled up my empty bag of M&Ms and tossed it in with the popcorn and soda cup.

"She did." He picked up my hand and kissed it in a very

gentlemanly fashion.

I smiled. "You know what I mean. Before you met me. Were you ever serious about someone else?" The lights in the theater flickered on, and I squinted in the brightness.

A clouded look crossed his face. "There was someone, but that was a long time ago."

"What was she like?" We got up and scooted out into the aisle, bringing our garbage along with us.

"I don't really want to talk about it."

"Why not? Did she break your heart?" I teased.

As we headed toward the exit, he grew quiet.

Serious now, I asked, "Did she?"

"I met her in college. We dated for three years. I thought I loved her." He held the exit door open for me and tossed our garbage into the can by the door. "We got engaged after graduation. We were going to get married after I finished grad school." The door slammed behind us, and we headed for James's car parked around the corner of the building. "She worked as a nurse at the VA hospital. The nightshift. We barely saw one another. Then, one day, I came back to our apartment for a paper I had forgotten. I caught her in bed with another guy." He pressed the alarm button on his car key and opened my door for me.

"Oh, honey, I'm so sorry. That must have been terrible." I slid into my seat and waited for him to climb in the driver's side.

When he got in the car, he put the key in the ignition without starting it. "He was a doctor on staff. Older, married. She told me later it had been a fling, a mistake, she said. But I ended it. I broke off the engagement, moved my stuff out, and never saw her again—end of story. I guess I wasn't ready to trust someone else like I trusted her. You don't know what it's like—to be lied to, deceived. I never wanted to feel that way again. But then, I met you."

"What's so different about me?"

"I don't know—seeing you with that flat tire. You looked

so frustrated, and cute, and—" His green eyes lit up, and he pulled me in close to him, kissing me lightly on the nose.

"No need to explain." I curled up against the warmth of his body, the emergency brake getting in the way. "I don't care why. I'm just glad you rescued me that night or we might never have met."

"Just call me James the Gallant, Rescuer of Beautiful Women in Need of Spare Tires."

"You mean, I'm not the only one? There's other women out there who have experienced the magic of your tire changing skills?"

"I don't share the magic with just anyone."

"Are you sure?"

"I'm sure." He kissed me, pressing his lips to mine, thrusting his tongue with gentle warmth into my mouth.

James the Gallant had rescued me that night, and I couldn't have imagined meeting a more loving man than he. I lost myself in that kiss, and swore silently that I would never hurt him as he had been hurt before. I knew what I had, and I didn't want to screw it up.

*

Joaquin pulled up to the valet parking sign outside the restaurant, the engine purring in neutral. My gaze froze on the back of his neck: short, clipped hair on dark, smooth skin. I used to wrap my arms around that neck, and now I would do anything never to see it again.

Janice turned around to face me. "What's wrong, Suze? You look positively ill."

Joaquin, handing his keys to the valet, didn't hear our little exchange of words.

"Too many margaritas," I confessed, hoping she would believe me. "And all that vodka. I guess I need to eat something."

"Well, let's get inside, then."

Joaquin opened the passenger's side door for her.

"What a gentleman." Janice took the offer of his hand to help her out of the low-slung car.

His perfect teeth glittered in the dusk. *"De nada,"* he rumbled.

Watching him from the back seat, I could imagine the young man he used to be. How he had charmed me with his good looks and confidence the very first time I met him. But now I could see the charm wasn't just for me. He poured it on for Janice, too. Had he acted this way when we were dating? I couldn't remember very clearly. But I could remember those hands on my body and his full lips kissing mine.

My body flushed at the memory.

Funny how some details I could never forget, but others were so elusive.

Before he could turn his attention on me, I pulled on the door handle. Joaquin had his hand on the small of Janice's back, guiding her toward the sidewalk and the benches outside the restaurant entrance. I took the opportunity to get out of his car and step up onto the curb unassisted.

At the click of my sandals on the concrete, he looked over Janice's shoulder and frowned. I didn't care. So I looked the fool for not waiting for his escort. Or possibly made him the look the fool. I couldn't be sure. Tonight would be hard enough without obsessing over these small details.

"Señor Hernandez, bienvenidos." A short man in a dark suit greeted us at the entrance. Clearly, Joaquin dined here often. I wondered what other women he may have entertained. Unwanted jealousy pricked my heart.

Why should I care what Joaquin had been up to all these years? I had left him hanging. He had every right to move on with his life, meet other women. But for some reason, I didn't want to be rational.

I needed to call James when we got back to the hotel room. At that moment, I wished for his voice in my ear. James had shared everything with me: his childhood, his previous relationships, his hopes and fears. I knew him better almost than I knew myself, and he thought he knew me. I wanted to confess it all to him. Reveal I was married to a man I hardly knew anymore. I wanted to believe James would forgive me.

But what if he didn't?

That one niggling doubt kept me here at the restaurant, even though I wished I were a million miles away. What if, when James heard the truth, he left me? His heart had been badly broken once, and it took him years to get over it.

If he found out about my lies, would he still trust me? Would he still love me? Would I be just another woman who broke his heart?

I couldn't bear the thought of it.

I steeled myself for the coming evening. Waiting for the bombshell to drop and for Janice to declare our friendship over, my engagement a farce, and my life one big lie.

Oddly enough, it never did drop.

*

Somehow we made it through dinner without one word about our dating history or our marriage. Joaquin must have sensed Janice's ignorance of this fact, as he, too, chose to keep silent on the topic.

He had gotten us the table with the best view in the place: right in front of a huge set of French doors that opened out to a balcony. We overlooked the mouth of the bay and all of Acapulco to the south. The lights sparkled and reflected off of the black waters in a breathtaking sight. Joaquin sure knew how to impress.

"So, were you surprised, Suze?" she asked me, all smiles and giggles. As if she had really pulled one over on me.

Oh, if she only knew.

"Oh, yeah, you got me good. I didn't expect to see Joaquin here."

"I know. I couldn't help myself." She unfolded her white

dinner napkin and set it on her lap. "I mean, I wanted to come back to Mexico, but never in a million years did I think we would run into Joaquin!"

The host at our table smiled. "I assumed the last time I saw you," he looked pointedly at me across the table, "would be the end our friendship. But imagine my shock when Janice called a few weeks ago to let me know about your plans."

"Yes, imagine the shock." I took a sip of wine.

Janice didn't seem to notice the tension in the air. "And he's been so nice about setting everything up—giving us one of the best rooms. Such great service. Everything's so perfect."

"I'm glad you are enjoying your stay so much already." He patted her hand in a friendly gesture. "It's the least I can do for two beautiful ladies."

"Your hotel is fantastic. The food, the service, the suite— everything," she declared, taking a drink of wine. Having Janice there made light conversation easy. "We signed up for the kayaking, but I want your opinion, Joaquin. Which would be more fun: the kayaking class or windsurfing?"

"I didn't think Susie was the adventurous type." He eyed me over the rim of his wineglass.

"She's more into practicing her volley on the tennis court, but she promised she would do whatever I wanted on this trip. Right?"

"Right," I said.

"Even if it means she has to learn to do tricks on a trapeze—"

"Not that again. Could you please explain to her what 'closed for safety reasons' means?" I looked at Joaquin. Keeping the topic of conversation off of the past was vital. I would do anything to distract Janice from our days as foreign students in Mexico and my history with Joaquin.

"I'm sure it's nothing," she countered.

"Tell that to the guy they probably have stashed away at the local hospital with a broken pelvis," I said.

A white-coated waiter arrived at our table with a tray

weighted down by plates and steaming food.

"Ladies, our meal has arrived," said Joaquin. "We will have to continue this debate later."

The waiter set a plate in front of me laden with meats, a variety of *mole* sauces, and piping hot corn tortillas. I got in one last jab, "I'm *not* learning how to do flips twenty feet in the air."

"But you promised." Janice dug into her food. Not even a friendly argument could stop her from eating.

"That was before I knew resorts were turning into circus training camps."

"Enough, you two." Joaquin held his hands up between us like a referee in a boxing match. "We can discuss this later, no?"

Janice spent the rest of the meal prodding Joaquin for ideas about places we should visit and things we should do during our stay. Things that didn't include trapezes or bodily harm of one form or another, thank goodness. The light banter made it easy to forget the tension from earlier that evening. Having Janice there kept the atmosphere superficial. Joaquin was an old friend and nothing more. How easy to convince myself of that when downing delicious Mexican cuisine I didn't have to pay for.

As we waited for coffee and dessert, Janice excused herself to the ladies' room. I knew she hoped I would come along so we could gossip about my old boyfriend, but I saw this as the opportunity to talk to Joaquin in private, even if only for a few minutes.

The moment Janice left the table, my nerves returned.

"So, you decided to come back to your husband? Ready to play wife now?" All friendliness and light had gone. Joaquin shifted from first gear into third without using the clutch.

I hadn't prepared for such a quick onslaught. "That's not fair, Joaquin. You don't have any idea what happened, why I chose to do what I did." My stomach twisted into knots.

"No, you're right. I don't." He picked up his wine glass and swished around the last few sips of his chardonnay. He paused for a moment and assessed the color of the drink in the candlelight. "So why don't you tell me all about it? You had cold feet? You wanted to run home to your mother? You had a boyfriend back in the States, and I was your fling?"

His last comment struck close to the truth. Close enough, anyway. I didn't have a boyfriend back then, but I had one now, a fiancé who loved me and who waited for me to come home to him. I didn't want to make things worse by bringing up James, however. "That's not it at all."

He set his glass on the table.

"I loved you, Joaquin, I really did."

"Loved?"

"Yes, I did." I let that sentence sink in. "But I was young, we were only nineteen. I didn't know what I wanted."

"And you do now? After hiding for how long?" Before I could answer, he pushed his plate aside and narrowed his eyes. "This meeting was no surprise."

"What do you mean?"

"You chose Acapulco—my hotel—for a reason." He stroked his goatee.

"No, that's not true. Janice made all the arrangements. I had no idea that you—"

"She's your little helper. You couldn't face me alone, so you had to drag her along."

"It's not that at all," I sputtered, but the truth seemed so ludicrous. Janice picked this place, not me. But why would he believe me? After everything I'd done to him, I didn't blame him for being suspicious.

"Then, please, tell me how it is, Suzie. Clearly, I can't figure it out for myself." He leaned back against the soft cushions and crossed his arms.

"Did you guys miss me?" Janice appeared at the table.

The tension hung thick in the air. Joaquin managed a friendly smile, and the hard line of his jaw softened ever so slightly—he returned to being the congenial, old friend once again. As if nothing had transpired between the two of us.

"Ah," exclaimed Joaquin as our waiter approached, tray in hand. "Here is our dessert."

Although my mood had soured, I took a spoonful of flan and listened as Janice and Joaquin continued their earlier discussion about tourist attractions in Acapulco. What a different dinner this would have been if Joaquin and I were just old friends. I envied Janice's relaxed demeanor, the questions asked with a wide smile of pleasure, the dessert eaten without the twinge of bitterness in her stomach.

I pushed aside my plate, and thought of tomorrow and the phone calls I needed to make. The candles flickered in the light wind that blew through the open French doors, and I looked out over the darkened bay, my thoughts swirling in my head.

Chapter Five

I remembered the day I met Joaquin—the day that started all of this in motion. It had been dusty, dry in Puebla, Mexico. Janice, Mercedes, and I stood in the hot sun, bags sitting in the dust at our feet, right near the gated entrance to the university where we were attending school as foreign exchange students.

"Hitchhiking? In Mexico?" Janice squawked. "Nobody's hitchhiked safely in the United States since, like, 1950 or something."

When Mercedes, my Mexican roommate, invited Janice and I to visit her family in Mexico City, we assumed we would be going by bus. Traveling by bus in Mexico was cheap, but Mercedes told us the buses were too slow. If we went by bus, we wouldn't reach the city until dark.

She convinced us of another, faster way to travel. And we trusted her—up until now.

"We do it all the time here," Mercedes said. "I wouldn't hitchhike on the road, but right by the gates?" She gestured at the eight-foot-tall iron gates that protected the entrance to the school. A small building between the gates housed the guards who checked the IDs of all car and foot traffic coming onto the school grounds. "It's perfectly safe."

Without waiting for us Americans to be convinced, she waved at a small brown sedan that pulled up to the gate. As the driver waited for the guard to allow him to exit university property, Mercedes approached his passenger side window.

Flashing her most winning smile, Mercedes tapped gently on the glass. The young man inside leaned over and rolled down the window to get a look at the attractive girl.

Mercedes eyes lit up when she saw the driver. Did she know him? She leaned inside the car and kissed the driver soundly on each cheek. Definitely not a stranger.

I couldn't hear a word she said, but her smile grew bigger and her head bobbed with excitement.

A quick nod told us this guy would graciously take on three female passengers. "Come on! Get in. This is an old friend of mine from high school. He won't bite." Mercedes grabbed her bag from the pile in the dirt and climbed in the front seat.

Janice looked over at me, "Well, if he's a friend of Mercedes—"

"That's true." I tried to get a glimpse of the driver through the glare of the windshield. How providential that this guy happened to be visiting *Universidad de América Central* on the day we needed a ride to the city.

"I'm sure he's a nice guy." Janice picked up her bag and climbed into the back of the car.

We both looked forward to a weekend away from the small campus. Most foreign students spent weekends in the dorm, doing homework or sticking together like a bunch of scared rabbits. How were we supposed to soak up any Mexican culture like that? We had made a pact before we decided to study abroad that we would make the most of our time here in Mexico. Here was our opportunity.

Janice and I had had enough of sitting together in the cafeteria on a Saturday afternoon or aimlessly wandering the campus. We wanted to experience new things. Mercedes had offered us that chance.

My bag looked lonely there in the dust, so I picked it up

and carried it toward the car.

Mercedes, smiling in the front seat, laughed at something the driver said to her. Because of the glare, I couldn't get a good look at our chauffeur. But seeing the gleam in Mercedes dark eyes and how she swept her long, thick hair off the back of her neck, exposing the soft nape to the warm air, this was no ordinary high school buddy driving the car.

As soon as I clanged the door shut, the driver sped out of the university gates and headed toward the nearby freeway. Without any air conditioning in the car, we rolled down every window to let in the breeze. This made it impossible for Janice and I to hear much of the conversation going on up front, but we could talk without anyone overhearing.

Janice made the first observation, "He's gorgeous!" She didn't seem to care, either, if anyone noticed her staring at the driver's profile. If he turned his head, he would surely see the unadulterated lust in her eyes.

"Is he?" At that moment, I looked up at the rearview mirror, hoping to see at least one little feature reflected there— a nose, an eye—anything.

He looked right at me!

I blushed and looked away, but not before I got a good look at his face.

He was startlingly handsome. Most Mexicans I had met so far were traditional *mestizo* in looks: short, broad nose, very dark skinned, slight of build. His skin, instead of burnished bronze, was a warm honey color, and his eyes were a greenish hazel and were wide-set.

Since I arrived in Mexico two months ago, he was the first Mexican male to catch my attention. I had a feeling he knew it.

Mercedes, knowing our Spanish to be rudimentary at best, turned to give us the basic facts of our driver. "This is Joaquin. He was visiting a friend at our university, and now he's on his way home."

"Hi, I'm Suzie, and this is Janice,"

He smiled a toothy smile that I could see reflected in the

rearview mirror.

"Do you always pick up strange girls on your way home?" I asked.

"Strange girls?" Joaquin looked back at the highway in front of him. "Who said you were strange?"

Mercedes pushed him lightly on the shoulder, laughing at his joke. "Oh, don't listen to her. We're grateful that you picked us up. If we had taken the bus, we wouldn't have gotten to the city until late."

Joaquin looked directly at me when he responded, "And then you would have to take the Metro—three beautiful *señoritas* at night on the Metro? Not such a good idea, eh?"

I had a hard time following the conversation from the back seat with the wind blowing loudly into the car. Looking out the window, I watched the countryside go past. High above us stood the magnificent Mount Popocateptl, a volcano that hadn't erupted in years. It was the highest point in the range of mountains that ringed Mexico City to the south. With snow on its crown most of the year, it formed a perfect pointed peak. From the university we had a clear view, and it made for the most spectacular sunsets.

"Don't you think he's cute?" Janice asked me.

"I guess so, if you're in to that type of guy."

"What type of guy? Gorgeous, tall, and muscular?" She rolled her eyes at me, as if I were a fool.

Joaquin said in his fluent, yet accented, English, "Hey, no secrets back there. It's three of you against one of me."

He turned his head to talk over the seats, and I got a good look at what Mercedes drooled over. His profile was even better than what I had seen in the rearview mirror.

Mercedes drew Joaquin's attention back to her, using her one advantage over us: Spanish. She sped up the conversation, knowing Janice and I wouldn't be able to keep up.

I leaned back and looked over at Janice, "Can I borrow one of your CDs?" I pointed at her bag on the floor by her feet. Might as well make the time pass. It would be too hard to try to keep up a conversation from the back seat.

"Sure." She handed me the whole bag, and I unzipped a side pocket where Janice usually kept a few CDs for traveling.

"Thanks." I grabbed the first case I saw and put the disc into my CD player. As music filled my headphones, I slipped into a comfortable state—staring out the window at the passing scenery and trying to keep my thoughts off the beautiful man sitting in front of me.

*

"*Quieres una torta?*"

The deep, male voice startled me out of a restless sleep.

For a moment my mind couldn't comprehend what he asked me. I rubbed my eyes and pushed a sweaty strand of hair out of my face, "Huh?"

"He wants to know if you're hungry. We stopped at a *torta* stand." Janice jabbed me in the ribs.

I pushed her hand away and straightened up, embarrassed that I had been caught sleeping.

Joaquin leaned against the side of his car, squinting at me in the late afternoon light. I looked out the open window and saw a small wooden kiosk with a colorfully painted sign above it—*TORTAS, TAMALES, LICUADOS.* The hot pink and fluorescent yellow lettering glowed as brightly as any neon sign.

"*Quieres?*" Joaquin questioned me again.

I got my first good look at our driver. He was physically imposing, leaning there. Broad-shouldered and muscular with a brilliantly white smile—I had a hard time resisting him.

Mercedes waited in the short line in front of the *torta* stand.

"*Sí, por favor,*" I reached for my money in my purse, as did Janice.

He put up his hand in protest, "No, no, I will pay for it." He lazily pushed off from the car and joined Mercedes in line.

He knew I was watching him, arrogant bastard. *But a fine-looking bastard.*

I had never encountered a man with so much self-confidence—as if he expected me to be attracted to him. For a moment, I wanted to brush off his charm and ignore his flirtations. But why not have some fun?

Here Janice and I were in Mexico, an exotic foreign country with an exotic foreign man. No one back home would ever have to know about him. Why couldn't I put aside my doubts about his intentions and have a good time with it? Who cared if I was another girl in a long line of girls? Sometimes you had to let go and let things happen.

I got out of the car and held the door open so Janice could slide across the seat and follow me. My eyes stayed on Joaquin's back.

"God, I'm starving."

Janice interrupted my wayward thoughts.

"Me, too," I said distractedly.

The focus of my concentration was not hard to notice.

"See! I told you he was gorgeous," Janice smiled triumphantly.

"When you're right, you really get it right." Smoothing back my hair and straightening my clothes, I walked up to the two of them standing in line. Janice followed hot on my heels.

"I don't feel right about you buying us dinner after giving us a lift into the city. Here," I pressed some pesos into his hand, "Please take this." That small gesture gave me the opportunity to lightly brush his palm with my fingers, a lingering touch. He took the heavy coins from me.

"You know what this means," he said. "Now, I will have to buy you and your friends a drink."

"What do you think, girls?" I smiled at Mercedes, "Should we take him up on his offer?"

"We might be able to meet you tomorrow night," said Mercedes.

Janice beamed. She'd wanted to make a trip to the *Zona*

Rosa in downtown Mexico City ever since we arrived. The *Zona Rosa* took up an area several blocks long in the center of the city where nightclubs and discotheques thrived.

Joaquin directed his words at me, as if I were the only one standing there on that street corner. "*Club Azteca.* Nine o'clock?"

I hesitated.

Janice poked me in the back.

"Why don't I give you my number, and you can give me a call if you decide to go." He grabbed a napkin from the small counter in front of the *torta* stand and looked to me to provide the writing utensil. I reached into my purse and pulled out a pen. "My friends and I usually meet there on Saturdays." He scribbled some numbers down.

I took the paper from his hand and tucked it in the back pocket of my jeans.

"Why don't you two wait in the car? We can get the food," said Mercedes.

I twisted my hair into a knot at the back of my head and let the evening air cool my sweaty neck. I nodded, and Janice and I went back to the sedan. From the backseat, I watched Joaquin and Mercedes as they shared the burden of carrying our food. They looked good together, their dark heads touching as they added more *chiles* to their *tortas* and grabbed extra napkins.

Then, Joaquin turned and caught my eye, his face spread with a glorious, white smile. I had never seen a man more handsome than that very moment on the side of the road outside Mexico City, the dust blowing around our feet.

*

"*Hola, bonita. Bailamos?*" A tall Mexican approached me in the dark at Club Azteca.

Flashing, colored lights dipped and twirled above the dance floor, but the ambient lighting near the bar and tables was almost non-existent.

Even in the dark, I recognized the tilt of his head, the wideness of his shoulders. Joaquin. He had come, and I didn't see any friends with him.

The music blared in Spanish. Tunes I did not recognize, but with an infectious beat.

Janice encouraged me, "Go on, dance! Mercedes will be back in a little awhile."

Joaquin stood in front of me, waiting for an answer to his question: Would I dance with him?

I looked up at him, his face shrouded in shadows, and nodded my assent. My breathing quickened in anticipation of his hands on my body.

He grasped my hand and possessively curved his other arm around my waist. His touch burned, and I leaned into him, enjoying the feel of his body next to mine. Guiding me to the dance floor, we swayed to the Latin beat of the music.

"*Cómo estás, bonita?*" His eyes were warm, his lips sensuous and full.

"*Bien,*" My stomach bubbled over with excitement. "*Y tú?*"

"*Muy bien.*" He drew out those two words, and his eyes sparked at me. The attraction between us was stronger than anything I had ever experienced.

We shifted and moved to the music, song after song. An instant chemistry sparked between us. Something gnawing and fierce.

We danced through a whole set of songs. I paid no mind to how long I had been in his arms.

Someone touched my shoulder.

"Why don't you give someone else a turn?" Mercedes butted in.

Instead of ignoring the rude interruption, Joaquin welcomed the battle over his attentions. A slight, sardonic smile appeared on his face. What red-blooded male doesn't enjoy the possibility of a cat fight?

He dropped his hand from my waist and stepped back,

waiting.

I wanted to shove her away, tell her in no uncertain terms that Joaquin had asked *me* to dance and not her. But a fleeting thought crossed my mind: once the weekend ended, we would be back at school sharing a dorm room. I had seven more months in Mexico, and I wanted to enjoy them. I stepped away from Joaquin.

When Mercedes stepped into his embrace for her dance, I gave Joaquin a slow smile, letting him know I would be waiting for him once the music ended.

They disappeared into the crowd of dancers, enveloped in mass of swirling skirts and dark heads.

Chapter Six

"Wake up, sleepy head!"

I groaned and rolled over, covering my head with a pillow. Who wakes up this early in the morning on a vacation?

"Come on! Kayaking class starts at nine, so we only have two hours to get ready and eat breakfast," Janice announced, more chipper than any human being should be at seven in the morning.

Uncovering one eye, I squinted from my pillow cave. "Five more minutes?" I begged.

"No, no, no, Suze," Janice scolded, pulling the pillow off me and folding down the covers. "We can't be late for our very first lesson."

I turned over and propped myself up on my elbows. "Hey! You're already dressed!"

Janice wore her bikini top, a pair of khaki shorts, a stripe of zinc oxide on her nose, and her straw hat now bedecked with a small Mexican flag tucked in the band. "I've been up since five-thirty."

Although exhaustion weighed me down, I couldn't help but be caught up in Janice's enthusiasm. She was the bright light in a dark room for as long as I had known her. She had never been afraid to try anything once, with the exception of second dates.

I swung my feet over the side of the bed. "All right. I'm up."

Janice beamed.

"Give me coffee and fifteen minutes, and then we're out the door."

"Ten."

"Twenty!"

She laughed. I loved her hoarse honk of a laugh. I smiled, rubbed my eyes, and scampered off to the bathroom for a quick shower.

"There'd better be coffee when I get out of here!" I yelled.

"A good dip in the ocean should wake you up!"

Kayaking? I must be crazy.

*

"And that ends the safety portion of our course," said our instructor, a short but well-built native with only a touch of an accent.

During the half-hour lecture, Janice sat, listening intently. If she thought to bring along a notebook, she probably would have filled it with notes. She took her sports seriously.

I, on the other hand, had a difficult time keeping my mind on the endless list of what-to-dos and what-not-to-dos, the details of the equipment, the demonstrations. I was more interested in observing the rest of our class: one man.

Our introductory sea kayaking lesson included three people: me, Janice, and a stocky fellow named George. I wasn't sure if I should be worried (why did no one else want to take this class?) or happy. Less people meant more one-on-one instruction, right? Maybe we could get through all the basic maneuvers more quickly with only three participants.

When the instructor handed me a life jacket, a helmet, and a paddle, I wished I'd listened more closely to his lecture.

First, we were to practice paddling, and then, we needed to try rollovers.

Rollovers looked to me as if they were paid underwater torture sessions. Our instructor had taught us to sit in the kayak, flip upside-down, and then right ourselves and our kayak in one smooth motion. I had not been known for doing anything in one smooth motion.

Janice's eyes lit up at the thought; my stomach heaved. Feeling lightheaded, I plopped down on the slick boards of the pier.

"Are you all right?" our classmate, George, asked. He reached out a broad hand to help pull me up from the ground.

Regaining my feet, I smiled weakly at him, "I guess you could say I'm scared out of my wits."

Janice threw an arm around me and gave me a reassuring squeeze, "Oh, Suze, you'll be fine. You know how to swim, so what is there to be scared of?"

"Getting trapped underwater and drowning?" I answered.

George, who was fast becoming my new best buddy, slapped his helmet down on his head and declared, "I'll go first." Then, he winked at Janice and me.

Janice's face flamed red—she blushed!

Our instructor assisted George in climbing into his kayak and getting him seated properly. Then, I prayed to God George would come back to us in one piece.

Janice must have had the same thing on her mind: George, that is.

"Mmm, he seems nice."

"Who? Enrique?" I squinted at our no-nonsense instructor.

"No, silly!" Janice blushed again. She pressed one hand to the top of her floppy hat to keep the stiff breeze from blowing it away. I wondered what would happen to her hat when the time came for her to put on a kayaking helmet.

"Huh?" My mind focused on the status of her hat rather than her statement about an attractive man.

"George," she whispered urgently, watching him practice

his paddling. "He's not quite my type of guy, but—"

"Your *type*?" I had no idea this woman had *any* type at all. Then, I thought about it some more. "Well, he is a little on the short side." And I was being kind. George stood about five-feet-five and had a barrel chest, your typical Greek-American.

"Oh," Janice answered, as if she hadn't noticed that particular glaring fact. "I meant his interests. I mean, river rafting is fun and all, but is that really a sport?"

River rafting? Did I miss something? How much zoning out did I do during that lecture, anyway?

"Hmm, yeah, I see what you mean." *Good cover, Eisenhart.* "But I think lots of rafters take it very seriously."

"You do?"

"Yeah. Wasn't it one of those Olympic demonstration sports last summer?" Now I was on a roll.

"It was?"

"I think so." So, Janice liked George, the short, Greek guy. Interesting couple they would make. Her, almost six feet tall and willowy as a reed; George much shorter and built like a tank. A match made in Acapulco heaven.

"Hmm—"

Time to push her out of the nest. "I think you should go for it."

"I should?"

"Yes. He's a nice guy, he's adventurous—"

"And he was very gentlemanly when he helped you up."

"Exactly." I saw Enrique approaching us with a now-drenched George, and I knew what I had to do. Time for me to be as good friend to Janice as she had been to me. I stepped forward and boldly announced, "I'll go next."

That should give those two plenty of time to get acquainted. She better thank me for this later.

My legs were jelly, but I strode toward the kayak bobbing in the ocean. Strapping the helmet on my head, I kept moving, worried if I paused for even a split second, I would lose my nerve.

"Now, if you need any kind of assistance, tap the top of your helmet twice, ok?" Enrique explained.

I nodded my head, but wondered to myself, if I tapped my helmet when I was trapped underwater, who would notice?

*

"Wasn't that a blast?" Janice asked me, her face still beaded with water from rollover practice.

I should have guessed she would learn kayaking with little trouble. I, on the other hand, coughed up sea water. I passed the basic skills exam at the end of class by the skin of my teeth. But I think Enrique let me pass because he felt sorry for me. My hair hanging in wet ropes, my limbs rubbery, and my waterproof make-up most likely smudged, I probably looked like a drowned rat.

From behind, I heard the slapping of feet on the wet boards of the pier. "Hey, ladies!"

It was George. He'd wanted to talk to our instructor after class, so we'd left him behind to get some lunch. Now it looked as if he wanted to join our little group.

My ploy worked, I thought, not without some satisfaction.

Janice used a towel to wipe the remaining drops of water from her face and then fluffed her short, damp hair with her fingers. I'd never seen Janice primp before. Usually she couldn't care less if she were sweaty or mussed up. She must really like this guy.

George caught up to us. "I'm taking you two to lunch."

"You are?" Janice asked.

Why did this girl have to answer statements with questions? He was a guy, he was cute—the answer should have been a resounding yes.

"We'd love to," I interjected. Might as well skip the hemming and hawing that would inevitably ensue if I left Janice in charge of the conversation.

George smiled broadly and crooked his arms, giving us

52

each one to hold on to. "Then, shall we?"

Janice linked her arm with his, and I did the same. As he led us in the direction of the hotel, I had a brilliant idea.

"Oh, no!" I gasped, doing my best to sound disappointed.

"What is it?" Janice looked at me.

"James. I told him I would call again today. He'll think I forgot all about him." This actually was true. We got home late last night after our dinner with Joaquin, so I'd never even bothered to check if he'd left a message. This morning, Janice got me out of bed so early, my brain only thought about coffee and a shower.

"Yes, James," my friend echoed sadly. "Guess we should go back to the room instead."

"Huh?" I couldn't believe she didn't take the ball I was handing her and run with it. "No, no! You go ahead with George. I'll catch up in a bit. All right?" Good thing I was around to help her out. This girl had almost no instincts when it came to men.

"If you're sure—" Her eyes lit up, and her pencil-thin mouth turned up in a slight smile.

"Of course I'm sure." I pulled myself out of George's grasp.

"Good, it's decided then," George said. "We'll meet you in the café later?"

"You got it," I grinned back at them, an oddly well-matched couple.

As they strolled away, I watched them together for a moment. George with his swarthy appearance and stocky, but muscular, build; and Janice with her pale complexion and slight, athletic figure. A light appeared in Janice's eyes that I had never seen before. I would make sure to take my time joining them for lunch.

I made my way toward the north entrance of the hotel and the banks of elevators. It worried me I may have missed James's call. And what would he think when I didn't contact him by this morning? It was now well past noon, and he would be in the middle of his conference. I could try his cell, but he usually got so caught up in the computer displays and gadgets at those types of events that answering his cell phone would be the last thing on his mind. I'd be lucky if he even remembered to charge the thing.

Standing in the elevator, I decided to call his cell number first, and if there was no answer, call his room and leave a message. I could imagine him forgetting to check his cell phone for messages, but a red flashing light on the phone in his hotel room would certainly get his attention.

The elevator stopped on our floor. I headed toward the suite. Someone tall in a finely-tailored gray suit stood outside our door knocking quietly. At first, I didn't recognize him from behind. Then, I heard his voice.

"Suzie, are you there?"

Joaquin, his broad shoulders straining at the fabric of his suit, leaned forward and knocked a little more loudly.

"Joaquin, are you looking for me?"

He turned, surprise reflected in his hazel eyes.

"Suzie, there you are." He straightened his perfectly-straight tie. His eyes slid over my bikini-clad body, and he raised an eyebrow in an appreciative gesture.

Suddenly aware of my stringy hair, damp with seawater, and my smudged make-up, I rubbed under my eyes with my towel and then wrapped it around my waist. Why did I care what I looked like in front of Joaquin? I didn't need to impress him anymore.

He cleared his throat. "We need to talk about last night. There are things we need to discuss."

Maybe he was thinking about divorce as well. Maybe he had someone else in his life, too. "I think that would be a good idea."

"Do you have any plans for lunch?"

I should have told him I did have plans—Janice and George were waiting for me in the cafe. Instead, I heard myself answer as if from a distance, "No, I don't have any plans."

I needed to talk to him as soon as possible about the

divorce, so calling James would have to wait. In a way, having lunch with Joaquin meant I was doing something for James and me, so any guilt quickly dissipated.

"Come, *querida*, we need to talk." He grasped me by the elbow, took the key card from my hand, and unlocked the door to our suite.

He guided me to the couch and sat me down. I shivered in the cool blast of air-conditioning.

He took a seat across from me in the wingback chair. "Why don't you change, and then we can go to lunch." His voice tumbled over my body in a husky whisper.

Even though my mind whirled with thoughts of divorce and James, something buried deep within me came to life and drew me toward Joaquin. He had every right to be angry with me last night—he was my husband and I left him behind. He must have seen the change in me, the softening of my gaze or maybe the looseness of my limbs. The sophisticated woman I had become receded into the shadows, and the young girl of twelve years ago surfaced eagerly.

"All right," I said.

Everything about him was so masculine—his broad shoulders, his lean torso, his well-trimmed goatee. Suddenly, I wanted to take a shower, clean off the brine of the ocean and maybe cool myself down a little. I felt very exposed sitting in my bikini on the couch.

"I'll hop in the shower and be out in a jiffy. Why don't you make yourself a drink?" I nodded at the stocked mini-fridge.

"Okay," Joaquin answered. He watched me cross the room with an odd intensity.

I broke my gaze with him and ducked into the bedroom to undress. Alone in the bedroom, I held my breath, waiting. When I heard the clink of ice on glass, I exhaled in relief.

What was I so scared of? He sat in the other room having a drink, and I would be in and out of the shower and dressed in a matter of moments. Then, we could find George and Janice and join them for lunch. There was nothing wrong in what we were doing. I didn't need to feel ashamed or nervous. Two old friends having a conversation, having lunch.

But if it was innocent, why did it feel so wrong?

*

I came out of the bathroom, a thick terry robe wrapped snugly around me.

I jumped at the sight of Joaquin staring at me from the bedroom doorway, his gaze burning. What was he doing in here?

"So, how long has it been? Ten years?" he asked.

"Twelve," I answered, nervous, unsure. "I—I'll be dressed in a minute." I reached for the door to show him I wanted some privacy.

Joaquin stopped me from shutting it. "I want some answers from you," he said, his gravelly voice on the brink of anger. "You are my wife. And I should have what is mine."

His gaze flickered over me, and then rested on my mouth. I knew what he wanted. My stomach fluttered, making it hard for me to speak. I should be outraged, I should shove him out the door, but I didn't. I couldn't. I froze to the spot, caught between wanting to flee and wanting to fall into his arms.

I knew, somehow, that something like this would happen the minute we stepped into the hotel room.

He removed his jacket, laying it across the bottom of the bed. "Why did you leave me, Suzie?" He asked me, loosening his tie. A flicker of hurt darkened his face for a moment. "Where did you go? I didn't know how to find you."

I had no answer for him. Standing there in my bathrobe, I could think of nothing but how handsome he looked and how much pain I'd caused him. We were husband and wife, and I'd vanished into thin air. I wanted to wipe away the fine lines that worry left on his face. Those were indelible marks I had caused.

He growled, "You are my wife."

I backed away from him and into the night table, this spark of anger scaring me. When he saw me start, he reached for me.

I cried out in surprise. Struggling against the iron grip that held my wrist, the knot on my robe loosened.

He pulled me close.

Though I was afraid, his nearness aroused me. A flush raced through me, prickling but warm. He bent his mouth down to mine and kissed me hard. The familiar taste of his mouth on mine made the years melt away. A spiral of heat grew inside me, and I kissed him back, nibbling on his lips, thrusting my tongue greedily into his mouth. The coals of a fire, almost gone dead, roared back to life. The kiss intensified, like a red-hot brand on cool skin.

A gnawing empty space inside me grew, needing to be filled, needing the touch of skin. I pulled my lips away from his and started unbuttoning his dress shirt, revealing a tan, hard chest. He quivered at the touch of my hand on the planed expanse of skin.

Joaquin pulled me in closer, my face hidden in his shoulder. "You are mine, *querida*. Didn't you know I wouldn't forget you?" he asked in a whisper.

He kissed my hair, the back of my ear, my throat. I was nineteen again and in love. Reaching up, I touched his face, and he muttered something in Spanish, nudging me toward the bed. He slid his hands up my neck to cradle my face. Hazel eyes scanned mine for a long second, perhaps to find something in them.

He leaned in, kissing me again, his sensual mouth tasting mine. My body was ripe, my limbs tingled in pleasure. I gave in to the ecstasy of the moment.

He pushed me down on the bed and tugged the robe from my body. The heavy material slipped from my shoulders, uncovering my most delicate parts. Girlishly, I tried to pull the edges back together. Joaquin brushed my hands away, drinking in my naked skin, my breasts warm and rosy, my stomach bare and trembling.

"You are so beautiful," he whispered against me, kissing each inch of skin he revealed.

Instead of feeling exposed, I bloomed under the heat of his gaze and the touch of his mouth. I was Venus arising from the sea, adored by all who saw me.

Arching my back, I reached again for him, thinking only of quenching the desire burning in me. All the years between us passed in an instant, and I remembered everything about him—the feel of his lips on mine, the coarse hair on his arms brushing across my body, the hardness of his well-sculpted chest against my softness. Familiar, yet unfamiliar. Time had changed us both, but yet we were the same.

His hand slipped between us and skimmed my naked hip, a touch as light as sunlight on water.

A clanging in my head snapped me back into the real world—this wasn't right. As much as the instinctual part of me wanted this coupling, the thinking part of me did not. I reached down to push his hand away, and at that very moment the phone rang.

The harsh buzz of the phone jolted us both. Joaquin's hand slid up to my waist, and his eyes, dark with desire, bored into mine. Our breathing ragged, we both sat unmoving, staring at one another.

When the phone jangled again, I rolled away from Joaquin and off the bed, quickly securing the bathrobe around me. I jerked the receiver off the phone and answered, "Hello?" My voice sounded taut and breathless.

"Suze, is that you?"

James.

Chapter Seven

I looked over my shoulder at Joaquin on the bed, resting on his elbows, his shirt loose and his belt unbuckled. Holding the phone to my ear, my mind was a blank. I felt sick to my stomach at what had happened, how far I let things go. What was wrong with me?

The question echoed in my head as I cleared my throat, hoping my voice sounded like good old Suzie. "Hey, honey! I was about to call you," I said, more weakly than I wanted. Without giving Joaquin another glance, I grabbed the whole phone and dragged it into the bathroom, shutting the door behind me.

"I got your message yesterday, but didn't want to call too late," he said. "Aren't you in a different time zone down there?"

James.

His voice, clear and steady, filled my ears, and it transported me back home to our little three-bedroom ranch right outside the city. We bought it together three years ago, right after I cancelled our first wedding date. I pushed him to buy the house to prove I honestly wanted to marry him. It was something permanent I could look at every day and think: here is *our* house with *our* garage and *our* half-dead lawn.

Now, I wished more than anything I'd never left that little green-and-white house in the cul-de-sac.

"I think we're one hour behind here, but I'm not exactly sure." I tried not to think about what waited behind that bathroom door—my shame, my guilt, my deceit. I told him with a lightness I didn't feel, "We went kayaking today. Can you believe it? Me, kayaking?"

How could I sound so normal? Talk about everyday things, as if nothing was wrong? James would know. He would sense my deceit. He knew me better than anyone.

"Kayaking?" James laughed. "That Janice, she always talks you into doing something crazy, doesn't she?"

"You know Janice. Never a dull moment with her." I stared at myself in the bathroom mirror, the slightest rash stood on my cheek where Joaquin's face brushed against mine when we kissed. I put my hand up against the reflective glass so I couldn't see myself. "Oh, hey, I think she might have met someone."

"A guy?"

"Of course a guy." I turned away from the mirror and sat on the edge of the tub.

"Hey, you never know when she might start pitching for the other team."

"James!"

He laughed, "Oh, you know I'm kidding, Suze. That's great she met someone. That doesn't leave you as the odd man out, does it?"

"No, she just met the guy today. His name is George, and he owns some kind of river rafting outfit in West Virginia."

"West Virginia? Are you sure he isn't engaged to his sister?" James guffawed at his poor joke.

Men and their sophomoric humor. "All right, all right. Enough teasing, hon. He's a good guy, and he really seems to like her."

"Good enough for me. As long as you don't run into any river-rafting studs, too."

My thoughts flashed to the half-naked man behind the bathroom door. A nervous laugh burst out of my mouth. "Oh, James, stop it. Hey, honey, I've been thinking about something ever since I got on the plane."

"You have?"

"Yes, when I get home, we are definitely going to pick a date for the wedding. And I'm sticking to it this time."

"That sounds like a plan." The happiness in his voice was unmistakable. "Maybe going to Mexico had been the right thing after all."

I thought back to a night several weeks before I left on this trip. The night my plans came together.

*

"Come on, Suzie!" Janice insisted over the phone. "You *have* to go with me to Acapulco. My Spanish is lousy, and it wouldn't be any fun for me to go alone. Plus, I'll pay for everything—all you have to do is say yes."

I *had* kept up my Spanish-speaking skills since college, that was true. Living in San Antonio I had plenty of opportunities to use it. But I didn't think James would be happy with me gallivanting around in a foreign country with an old college girlfriend. I was an engaged woman, after all. Plus, there were all those bad memories from Mexico—a marriage and a man I had been trying to forget.

"I can't. I'm sorry, Janice, but I've got so much going on at work. There's a new software product I have to document by the end of next month and some edits I've been doing for one of the other writers—"

"We're only going to be gone ten days, Suze," she begged. "I think your boss can manage without you for a week."

"And James would miss me," I countered, my resolve starting to break down. "He can't do laundry worth a darn. I know he'd be calling me all the time."

"So what if he calls?"

"I don't know."

"Think about it. Let me know by Friday, okay?"

"All right." Janice had the tenacity of a badger sometimes. My plan had been to avoid her altogether. If I didn't call her back by Friday, maybe it would be too late to book the flight or maybe it would be too expensive.

But Janice had other plans for me.

"Did you think I wouldn't let you go?" James asked me a few days later when I walked in the door after a late day at the office.

"Go? Go where?" My mind grew cluttered with the last minute details of a project at work.

"To Mexico? With Janice?" He handed me a plate of food—James was an excellent cook—and gently pushed me into a chair at the table in our kitchen.

Darn that Janice! "Oh." I lifted a fork filled with spinach lasagna to my mouth. I had a short reprieve from answering as I chewed the savory bite.

James hovered over me, waiting as I finished chewing and taking a long drink of milk. When I set my glass down he prompted, "Well?"

"I really didn't want to go, to tell you the truth. I tried to let her down easy." I quickly scooped up another forkful of lasagna.

"Why wouldn't you want to go? Half the time I'll be in Dallas." He studied me, then, seeing my blank look, prompted, "The convention?"

"I forgot."

"You forgot? I circled the dates in red on your calendar in your office, and you forgot?"

"What do you want me to say, James?" I sighed, setting my fork on the edge of my plate. "That I would love to go? That I certainly don't mind leaving my fiancé to go hang out with my single friend in Acapulco? In a bikini? With lots of unattached men around?"

"I think you should go."

"Really," I said, incensed.

"For our sake, I think you should go."

"What do you mean?"

"Suzie, how long have we been engaged?"

I hesitated, I hoped it wasn't the same conversation we had so many times before. "Four years."

"And how many wedding dates have we chosen?"

Yes, he headed into familiar territory. My heart sank. "Three."

"Three, Suzie. Three." He paced the kitchen as I watched from my chair at the table, my food now cold in front of me.

"So? What's so terrible about that?" I stood up to take my dish to the sink. My appetite had suddenly disappeared.

"I'm not getting any younger, Suzie. I want us to get married, you know that." He stopped his pacing and came to stand next to me by the sink.

We fell into our usual routine. I rinsed, he put the dishes in the dishwasher. We were quite a team.

"I know." I was ashamed of myself and ashamed of what I was doing to him. How much longer would he put up with me? What would be the last straw for him? I hated to think about it. I loved him, I really did, and I couldn't imagine not being with him. But some things couldn't be fixed so easily. If only I could get up the courage to tell him why I couldn't get married.

"I think you need to take this trip. I think we both need some time apart to think." James shut the door of the dishwasher with a click, then dried his hands on a towel hanging from the stove.

"We do?"

"Yes." He covered the remaining lasagna with tin foil. "I told Janice you were going. You're flying in to Acapulco and meeting her there."

"What?"

James placed the dish of lasagna in the refrigerator, closed the door, and headed toward the stairs, "She's buying your plane ticket tomorrow. You should probably call her so you two can make some plans."

He left me standing in the kitchen alone, my mind whirling. Was this an ultimatum? I wished I could be honest with him about why I'd put off our wedding so many times. If he knew the truth, he would've been easier on me.

The truth.

That's when the idea came to me. Why not confront my past and get that divorce. This trip could be my chance to fix things without hurting James. He wouldn't have to know. He would never have to know.

*

I wanted to keep talking. Keep that bathroom door shut as long as I could. Maybe if I stayed in here long enough, Joaquin would disappear, and I could pretend nothing ever happened. At that moment I'd gotten so far off course from my original plan, I couldn't see how I would be able to fix it.

While James told me about the cool little gadgets and computer programs he was fiddling with in Dallas, one part of my brain thought about what to do.

First, I would have to explain to Joaquin I had a fiancé and that episode on the bed had all been a mistake. Lust had taken over, memories of a past long over. Nothing more. Then, I needed to tell him I wanted a divorce. Maybe finding out I had a fiancé would put him off, make him angry enough to drop the intense looks, the heated touches.

From now on, no more meeting him alone. Clearly, that had been a bad idea. Next time I talked to him, I would pick a more public place—a restaurant, the hotel lobby, the beach.

"I miss you, honey," I blurted out. It was true. I did miss him. I missed his predictable, solid self next to me. When we were together I was safe, loved, appreciated. James would never do anything surprising or erratic. After four years together, I could read him like a book. Each little expression—a raised eyebrow, a cocked half-smile with his one dimple showing—

became a window into his mind only I could open.

"I miss you, too," James answered back.

I paused. I could hear only a bit of static on the line. I wanted to tell him more about this trip, but the words wouldn't come.

"Hey, look, Suze, when you get back, I think we need to have a long talk."

"A long talk? About what?"

"Us. You and me."

"You and me?"

Joaquin knocked on the door. "Suzie, are you coming out of there?"

Oh, God.

"What was that noise?" James asked.

"That? Oh, that was just Janice. She wants to know when I'll be off the phone." Panic rose in my throat. I tried to take a deep breath and calm myself. "We were about to go to lunch before you called."

"Suzie?" Joaquin called out.

"James, I really have to go. Why don't I try calling you again later?"

"Later? Okay. But tomorrow I'll be in presentations all day. Let's try for the day after tomorrow?"

"All right."

The knocking got louder.

"Love you, sweetheart," James said.

"Love you, too." I hung up the phone. I didn't want to open the door knowing Joaquin was behind it. What would I tell him? How could I explain my earlier behavior?

Best to get it over with quickly.

I unlocked the door.

Joaquin sat on the bed, his face clouded, shirt buttoned and tucked back in his pants. He reached for his striped tie and flipped up his collar.

"Who was that, Suzie?" He tied his tie, looping the end through the knot, then wiggling it upward to tighten it. After he folded his collar back down, he ran his fingers through his hair.

"It's a long story, Joaquin, but it's one of the reasons I came on this trip."

"Who was on the phone?" he demanded, anger and confusion plain on his face. When I didn't give an immediate answer, he made a grab for his suit jacket, his back to me.

"No one," I sputtered. "It was nobody."

"Nobody?" His back stiffened, and he half-turned his face toward me. "I see." He brushed imaginary lint off his jacket sleeve.

I needed to stop being such a coward. "It was my fiancé."

He turned to face me, his eyes dark and empty. "Your fiancé? So," he gestured to the crumpled sheets on the bed, "what was that all about?"

He had every right to be confused. I knew when Joaquin came into the bedroom James waited for me back home. He did not. He only knew his long-lost wife had returned. How could I blame him for picking up where we left off? I should have known better. I should have backed off immediately. In fact, I should have left him out in the hall.

I sunk, defeated, onto the bed pulling my bathrobe more tightly around me. "I'm not sure."

"You're not sure?" Joaquin growled. "I want to make love to a wife I haven't seen in twelve years..."

I cringed at those words. Those few lust-filled moments in bed had been shameful. That hadn't been like me at all.

He paced the room. "When we were having dinner last night, you never said anything to me about another man. Nothing."

"I know, and I should have."

"*Ay Dios*, you should have," he muttered. "You were *mine*, *querida*. When did you decide to give your heart away to someone else?"

"I know it doesn't make much sense to you. I had to leave. I had to go home. I left because my father died." The memory of my father's death now fresh in my mind. "My mother was a wreck, she could barely function. I couldn't bury my father and leave her there all alone."

"But why didn't you call or answer my letters?" he persisted. "Why didn't you tell me how to get in touch with you? Why you were gone? I would have understood. I would have come for you."

"No, you wouldn't have," I whispered, hiding my face in my hands. I couldn't handle the wave of emotions. Things I had wanted to forget bubbled to the surface.

"I wouldn't have? Who are you to decide what I might have done? You never gave me the chance!"

I looked up at him from my spot on the bed. "Your mother was so unhappy with me. It never would have worked. Can't you see that?"

"And when did you decide this? Before or after you met your new fiancé?" He returned to his pacing.

"Oh, Joaquin, that's not fair."

"Not fair? What would be fair, Suzie? You pledging yourself to me for eternity in front of a judge and then leaving me, taking off as if I didn't exist? How do you think I felt, Suzie? How do you think I *still* feel?" He stopped, and stood in front of me, arms crossed.

"I don't know, Joaquin. I have no idea how you feel."

"So, exactly why are you here? What do you want from me?"

"What we had, Joaquin, what we had all those years ago...those days are long past. You know that, I know that." I took a deep breath. "I've found the man I want to spend the rest of my life with. But I need a divorce. That's why I'm here."

For a long moment neither one of us spoke.

"It didn't seem to me that everything is in the past." He nodded his head toward the bed. "Can you honestly tell me you feel nothing for me now? Nothing but fond memories? Is that all?" He leaned against the bureau behind him, his muscular body masked under the suit jacket.

I let go of a ragged sigh. "That was a mistake. I just missed James is all. I lost my head for a minute. We have to forget it ever happened."

"*We* have to forget? Oh, no, *you* have to forget, Suzie, or you will drive yourself mad, won't you? Wondering if it's me you love or this James."

"I love James."

"Yes, so you told me. You may have forgotten, but I remember it."

"That's not fair Joaquin. Those days are long behind us."

"If they are so long behind us, then why did you kiss me like that? Why did you let me touch you?"

I pulled my robe a little bit tighter around my thighs, feeling naked under his penetrating gaze.

Joaquin smirked at me then, as if I'd made a joke and only he knew the punch line.

I grabbed some clothes out of my suitcase and pushed past him into the bathroom. "I have to meet Janice for lunch. She'll be wondering where I am. You can let yourself out." I trembled at the words, uncertain if he would be gone once I finished dressing. Part of me wished he would, but another part of me hoped he would still be waiting for me.

Five minutes later, I unlocked the bathroom door. Joaquin had vanished. I grabbed my purse from the night table and headed toward the door. When I reached it, my heart raced. To calm my nerves, I peered through the peephole. Not a soul in sight.

Joaquin had really gone, but the meetings were not over. I had only touched on the divorce. I would still have to convince him to go through with it. A battle I wasn't ready to wage just yet.

Chapter Eight

"My mother will love you," Joaquin tried to convince me a couple of months after we started dating.

"Are you sure? I'm an American. I thought she didn't like Americans." My nerves were edge as I sat next to him on the Metro, zooming through Mexico City. I was meeting his whole family that weekend. All of them. Three sisters, one brother, and his mother.

"I said she didn't like American food."

"The 'influence of America on Mexican cuisine,' I think was how you put it."

"That doesn't mean she dislikes American people."

"But it's one strike against me. My country brought pizza and fried chicken to Mexico. She'll never forgive me."

"It will be fine, Suzie. If she loves me, she'll love you."

"It doesn't always work that way, Joaquin."

"It will be fine. Trust me." He locked his fingers with mine.

"But remember what she told you when you wanted to study art?"

He set his mouth in a firm line and pulled my hand into his lap. "*Querida*—"

"She said you could find your own way to pay for it. That it would be a waste of her money. And she loved you then, didn't she?" I leaned my head against his shoulder. "What if she thinks I'm a waste of your time, too?"

"There's nothing to worry about. Nothing, okay?" He curled his arm across my shoulders, pulling me closer.

It would be a trial by fire: if I were serious about Joaquin, then I needed to meet her. Success, and we were destined to be together. Failure, and, well, I didn't want to think about failure.

We sat silently on the Metro for awhile. I watched the clutter of neighborhoods and people and cars fly by the window. Mexico City was a living, breathing being filled with activity, color, and noise. Taking it all in only added to my nerves.

As we got closer to Xochimilco, downright terror took over.

"What if she makes fun of my Spanish?"

"What?"

"Well, she doesn't speak English, and I'm not that fluent. What if she can't understand me?"

"I'll translate."

"But I want to be able to talk to her myself."

"She'll understand."

"How can she get to know me if you're translating everything?"

"Suzie, this isn't a test. You're meeting my family. You can't fail at this. Okay?"

"But it *is* a test. I could screw it up."

"You won't."

Joaquin squeezed my hand, and for a moment I forgot my worries and thought only of his beautiful body and his engaging smile. To know those things were only for me sent a shiver down my back. I could make it through this. I would make his mother love me. Just wait.

*

Joaquin lived at one end of the valley that cradled Mexico City, in the section known as Xochimilco. Made up of a twisted skein of canals, this section of the city was what remained of the main agricultural area of the Aztecs. *Trajineras*, special flat-bottomed boats, carried families, young couples, and friends on a slow journey down the canals providing food, drink, and souvenirs. Floating mariachi bands were the entertainment.

When we stepped off the train platform, the stairs led us right into the heart of everything. Smiling tourists, dancers dressed in traditional costume, and young children surrounded us.

A young woman approached bearing a basketful of long-stemmed roses, and Joaquin signaled to her. He gave her a few pesos and, smiling, took a rose from her basket and handed it to me.

This small gesture, this bit of velvet-red petals tightly closed together, touched me. Warmth unfurled inside me. It made me think: *this is first love, this is what it feels like.*

As I held the flower close to my chest, Joaquin led me through the maze of narrow streets to a broad, busy road. Clutching my hand tightly in his, he pulled me across when the traffic cleared. We only had a few moments before the cars closed in around us, and my heart pounded from the sudden movement, or maybe just from his hand being in mine.

He led me up a dirt path that skirted a steep embankment. All worries about meeting his family had since left my mind. I thought only of the flower, his hand, our feet. We scrambled together up that dusty slope and found ourselves on a large, flat piece of land. Adobe walls and makeshift fences lined the dirt roads. Rooftops and the wisps of trees peeked out from behind them.

"We're almost there," he said.

Nervous tension returned to trouble my stomach. I squeezed his hand.

"Do I look all right?" I touched my hair.

Joaquin stopped in his tracks, dropped my hand, and grabbed me by the shoulders, "You look *bonita, mi amor.*" The warmth in his voice and the sparkle in his eye made my doubts dissipate. "*Mi mamá*—my mother? She will adore you."

A few more blocks, and we were there.

The modest house was hidden behind an adobe wall with a wrought-iron gate. I saw his brown car parked in the small courtyard; it was the only car the family owned, so most of the time we had to travel around the city by Metro.

As he reached for the latch on the gate, I held my breath. A teenage boy peered out the window at us and then broke out in a smile. That had to be Joaquin's brother, Carlos.

The front door flew open, and a gaggle of young girls poured into the courtyard, squealing in Spanish. All of them had eyes on me as we came through the gate. I leaned in a bit closer to Joaquin.

The girls crowded around us like a swarm of bees, and the smallest one, who was ten or eleven, grabbed my hand, looked up at me, and smiled.

"*Qué bonita!*" Another sister commented, as if I were a pretty painting to be admired.

The oldest girl touched the fabric of my skirt, fascinated with it.

Spanish flew all around me, the girls chattering a mile a minute. Carlos hung back. He stood tall like his brother, but his eyes were a deep brown.

A lovely woman in her late forties appeared in the doorway of the house. It had to be Paloma, Joaquin's mother. Although she was a bit overweight, clearly in her youth she had been a beauty. She'd twisted her hair into an elegant knot. Her hazel eyes, so similar to Joaquin's, sparkled with life, and her fine features were smooth and youthful.

"*Bienvenidos a nuestra casa,*" she said succinctly. I knew Joaquin told her to speak slowly, so I could understand her.

"*Gracias.*" I held out my hand for a welcoming shake. Paloma, however, stepped forward, taking me into her arms and kissing each cheek.

I stiffened at the close touch of this stranger. This is not quite how we did things in my mid-western, uptight, suburban town. Paloma, too, seemed uncomfortable with the embrace, but she didn't let go.

When she pulled away, she had a grim look on her face. It made me pause for a moment.

She didn't like me.

Paloma took my bag from my limp hand and headed back into the house.

"Let me show you where you will be staying," she said in slow Spanish.

I looked at Joaquin, "I'm staying here at your house?" I wasn't sure I understood her.

He nodded. "Did you think I would let you stay in a hotel after you met my family?" A teasing note crept to his voice, as if I were being naïve for thinking his family would let me stay anywhere else but here.

Was that rude? To visit someone and not stay the night?

The sisters gathered around me like a gaggle of geese, each one wanting to take my hand and lead me inside. I followed them, trying to find out their names.

Joaquin had mentioned Carlos many times. They were both boys and only a few years apart, so perhaps he felt closer to Carlos. The girls generally were grouped together with the phrase 'my sisters,' as if they were all one entity. I had imagined three identical girls with Joaquin's hazel eyes, all with the dark brown, almost black, hair that most everyone had in this country.

But there couldn't be three sisters more different. Ana, the ten-year-old, had a reed-like figure with long beautiful fingers and waist-length hair twisted into two neat braids. Lupe, on the cusp of thirteen, had a short, square build and chin-length choppy hair. Claudia, the oldest sister, was also short, but had a thinner figure like Ana and wore heavy make-up and tightly curled hair.

I liked them all immediately, even though I couldn't catch more than one or two words of what they were saying. Their enthusiasm for a complete stranger coming to their home surprised and touched me. I felt instantly comfortable with these three girls, which more than made up for the cold reception from Joaquin's mother.

Ana took me up the narrow stairs to the bedrooms. "*Venga*, Soo-see."

The small house didn't suit so many people. Carlos and Joaquin shared a small room that rivaled the size of a walk-in closet in America. The girls had a larger room, but, because of my visit, Ana and Lupe would be sharing a bed.

My bag waited on the bed that would be mine, when Joaquin's mother leaned into the doorway.

"*Tienes hambre?*"

Nervousness had driven hunger out of me hours ago, but I nodded at the woman and her grim face. Her features hard as carved stone. I didn't want to appear ungracious and give her any more reason to dislike me.

*

Early evening arrived. The late afternoon meal had not gone well. The sisters talked over one another so much, I had a hard time following the conversation. I found myself tuning out what was going on around me due to a headache from concentrating on the buzz of voices. Instead, I studied my food and got a good look at the kitchen.

Paloma served beans and corn tortillas for lunch, with a sweet lemon tea. The beans came from a huge pot on the small stove behind the table. We each received a bowl with a soupy portion of beans, a large spoon, and a pile of heated corn tortillas.

The tortillas sat in the middle of the table under a damp towel to keep warm. Once we all sat down, a food free-for-all took place. Everyone at the table snatched tortillas from their heated spot under the towel and ripped them into small pieces. They used the small pieces to scoop beans from the bowl to their mouths. No utensil needed.

I couldn't figure out how they did it.

I tried to mimic their methods, but my piece of tortilla folded under the weight of the beans, and I only ended up with a soggy piece of the flat bread in my hand. Lupe, sympathetic to my problems, handed me a soup spoon. That made it easier to scoop the right amount of beans onto a large piece of tortilla, which I could then get into my mouth without too much of a mess. Ah, the poor American.

Paloma, sitting across the table, kept a close watch on me. Either she was judging me for my table manners or observing me with the keen interest any mother would have of her son's girlfriend.

After losing track of the thread of conversation yet again, I took a sip of my lemon tea and stared out the window at the bougainvillea that grew across the fence, its fuchsia blooms rippling gently on the breeze.

Paloma, apparently thinking my Spanish was so rudimentary I couldn't follow the simplest of phrases, asked Joaquin seated next to me, "*Ella puede entendernos?*"

Could I understand them?

My faced flushed at the insult. The cacophony of voices in the kitchen had made it hard to follow every sentence.

I answered in Spanish before Joaquin could defend me, "Yes, I can understand you. It's just difficult with so many people talking."

I wanted to explain why I may not have answered every question posed to me, but I think Paloma took it as an insult, as if I believed her family to be loud and rude.

Paloma's eyes snapped, but she remained quiet. She nodded and smiled, with the coldest, most unfeeling smile.

This meet-the-family thing was not going well.

For the rest of the meal, I did my best to respond to questions with very short answers.

Ana, the youngest and boldest of the three, asked me point-blank in Spanish, "So, you must be very rich, then?"

That question took me by surprise. What gave her the idea that I had a lot of money? I came here with a beat-up duffle bag and wearing clothes from Target.

"Uh," I hesitated, not knowing how to set her straight without making her feel ignorant.

But Joaquin spoke up for me, "Not every American is rich, *mensa*." He tugged affectionately on one of her long braids.

Ana blushed at her brother's teasing.

Claudia, fifteen and more mature, continued the line of questioning with a bit more finesse, "But I am sure you live in a bigger house and have your own car."

I thought of my parents sitting in the living room in our suburban home outside Chicago, the shelves filled with expensive knick-knacks, the large television off in the corner. My car, although a used one, was much nicer than the old brown sedan that played the role of family car at the Hernandez home.

"Yes, I do have my own car," I side-stepped the question about my parent's home, "but I paid for most of it myself by working after school."

I hadn't been entirely truthful; I had saved fifteen-hundred dollars from two summer jobs and planned to buy whatever I could afford. My father offered to pay the difference to get me into a newer, safer car.

Claudia nodded her head at that answer and then took another bite of tortillas and beans.

Lupe, her round face pleasant and sweet, asked the bombshell question, "So when you and Joaquin get married, are you going to live in Mexico or in the United States?"

Lupe asked this so innocently, as if she wanted to know if the weather would be rainy tomorrow or if my favorite flavor of ice cream was chocolate or vanilla.

At the time, I was taking a drink of lemon tea, and I choked on it. The burn of the liquid entered my lungs and caused a violent fit of coughing.

Paloma's eyes bored into mine.

I wiped the tears from my face. "What?"

Joaquin squeezed my hand and took over for me, "Lupe, why do you ask these things? It will only bother *Mamá*. She doesn't need this kind of worry."

For a moment, it seemed to me as if this discussion had already happened in this very room, with these same people.

Quiet Carlos saved the conversation by starting on a completely different topic: soccer. He and Joaquin spent the next ten minutes debating the different college teams and their chances in the next tournament. Paloma took this as her cue to stand up and start clearing the dishes away. The girls followed her lead, grabbing cups and plates, napkins and spoons. With so many women darting about the kitchen, cleaning up the mess from lunch, I felt out of place.

I had no interest in or knowledge of soccer, and Paloma had no need of my help. I sat at the table, watching as everyone in the family fell into their routines. But I had no routine. I had no place to go. I felt as if I were in the way.

Ana smiled at me as she swept my plate away, her braids bobbing. The girls liked me well enough, but not Joaquin's mother. When Lupe brought up the idea of Joaquin and I living in the United States, her bright, liquid eyes dulled for an instant. The faint lines on her face deepened and turned into dark furrows of worry.

I tried not to think about it. I wanted to spend time with my boyfriend and meet his family. We had no serious commitment between us. We had been dating less than two months, but for some reason, Paloma and her children thought something more going on. Had Joaquin given them that impression?

I stood up to get some air and to stretch my legs. As I passed Joaquin's mother at the sink, I politely said, "Thank you for a wonderful meal, *Señora*."

Paloma nodded at me, her eyes dark.

It had been a relief to escape the kitchen and those hazel eyes watching me.

Chapter Nine

"Where have you been?" Janice asked, not without a small amount of alarm. After all, we had parted ways outside the hotel over an hour ago.

I was surprised she and George still sat at the table in the cafe. Did I see one dessert plate with two forks sitting on the table between them?

"Well," I stammered, "I needed to take a shower." My damp hair hung heavily on my shoulders. "And James and I talked for quite awhile."

"James is her fiancé," she intimated to George who sat only inches from her in a very large booth. My absence had not been too much of a concern for the two lovebirds.

"Oh?" George took a forkful of some sort of ice cream concoction. "When are you two getting married?"

Janice, God love her, dove right into the answer, "They've had to cancel a couple of dates, but they're going to pick a new date soon."

"Mmm." George took another scoopful of dessert. "Are you going to be joining us?"

Looking at the two of them perched so cozily together, I wouldn't dare intrude. Considering my insides were a tight, roiling mass of worry, I wasn't in the mood to eat. "I'm really not that hungry." I stood awkwardly in front of their table as they sat facing one another, barely noticing my presence.

"Well," Janice began, "should I meet you somewhere later then?"

George's hand shifted closer to her thigh.

Time for me to vamoose.

"Sure. I could use a few hours of down time by the pool." It would be the perfect moment to sneak away and find out how to get a divorce rolling. How did one go about finding a lawyer in a foreign country? Did they have the Yellow Pages down here? Guess I could always try the Internet.

"Then maybe we could meet at the room later—for dinner," Janice glanced across the dessert dish at George, and he returned her look with an easy smile.

"Sounds good." As I said the words, I wondered if I shouldn't ask about George joining us. Maybe Janice needed a little help in getting over her shyness with men.

I shouldn't have been worried.

"I think George would like to join us, wouldn't you George?" Janice reached out and touched him gently on one well-developed shoulder.

"I'd love to." He looked at me. "That is, if it's okay with you, Suzie."

"Of course it's okay with me!" Who was I to stand in the way of true love?

"Hey, maybe we should make it a foursome and see if Joaquin wants to come along?" Janice suggested, stirring her iced tea with a straw.

"Well, I'm not sure if he can join us. He's busy, what with managing this place and all," I gestured limply at the half-full restaurant. Even *I* didn't believe what I was saying. Not as if the place would fall apart if he wasn't on hand every second.

"Why don't I give him a call?" Janice asked. "I'll see if he can come. Say, around 7:30?" She looked over at George.

"Sounds good to me," he said.

"I'll call him." Not a good idea to give Janice the opportunity to speak to Joaquin alone. "But I can't guarantee he'll be able to come."

"All right." Janice narrowed her eyes. "You're sure you don't mind calling?"

"Not at all. Joaquin and I go way back, remember? We're buds." I sounded like an eighteen-year-old stoner. Where in the hell was this coming from?

"If you're sure—"

"I'm sure. Not a big deal. I've got it all taken care of. You two enjoy the afternoon."

A few hours by the pool in the fresh air and sunlight sounded heavenly, but I had work to do. With a free afternoon when no one would question where I was or what I was doing, it would the perfect time to steal away, find out more about a quickie divorce, and get cracking on saving my future with James.

*

"And, so, you see, Ms. Eisenhart, there is no way you can do this alone and in only a few days. These things take time." The lawyer tapped a pencil on his desk to the beat of the salsa music drifting up from the streets through his open office window. "And you must talk to your husband before we can proceed with any legal action."

These were not the words I wanted to hear. I wanted *Señor Pablo Éstaban Esposito de Rincón, Esq.* to tell me I needed to sign a few forms. But according to *Señor* Esposito, even if I had every piece of paper work, every signature, to finalize a divorce in Mexico would take six months at the very least.

Six months I could wait. But having to talk to Joaquin again and beg him to sign the forms? That wouldn't be easy. He didn't seem to be in any big hurry to get rid of his long-lost wife judging from what happened between us earlier in the afternoon.

The pencil tapping grew more intense.

"Are you sure? Can't I just serve him with some paper or something?"

"Serve him?" Thankfully, the pencil tapping stopped at that question, and *Señor* Esposito sat up in his chair.

"Have the court send him the forms?"

"Ah. No, Ms. Eisenhart, this is not the United States, you know. There is no snapping of the fingers." He snapped his fingers in front of my face. "No instant divorce. Not any more. The Mexican government sees marriage as a serious contract between two people."

"I'd hoped, with the time constraints I have, that possibly—"

"That there would be another option?" He raised his bushy eyebrows.

"Exactly."

"There is no other option, except to remain married to your husband, of course." *Señor* Esposito went back to tapping his pencil in rhythm with the music.

"Oh."

The visit to the lawyer had not been as productive as I had hoped. Naïvely, I believed I could walk in the door as a married woman and walk out single. As much as I wanted to deny it, I would have to meet with Joaquin again and make him understand things were over between us, I had moved on with my life, and I needed a divorce from him. Right now.

If I stood my ground, didn't let his anger get to me or let my leftover feelings take control, it should work. Shouldn't it? Had it ever really been anything more than a marriage on paper? Joaquin would see that. The minute I explained it to him, he would see how we were truly never husband and wife.

The scene in the bedroom had been a fluke, a leftover echo of what we used to have together—nothing more.

*

Time had gotten away from me. The orange ball of the sun reflected in the swimming pool outside and reminded me of my dinner date with Janice and George. I'd forgotten to call Joaquin and invite him to join us.

My hand trembled as I held the courtesy telephone in the hotel lobby. It took me several tries before I could get up the courage to ask the receptionist to connect me to the hotel manager. My body flashed hot and cold as I waited for the series of rings on the other end.

One ring. Two. Three.

I anticipated the switch to a voicemail message and wondered if I should leave a message or hang up.

"*Bueno?*"

His voice again—the deep, rumbling voice that brought me back to those warm and sunny days years ago that I spent in his arms. My words caught in my throat.

"*Bueno?*" His voice more insistent this time.

"It's me."

"Suzie," he said flatly. "What is it?"

He didn't sound interested in talking to me at all. Not that I didn't expect that kind of response after the way we'd left things earlier today. But I had to try. I didn't come all this way to fail. James deserved my best efforts to fix my mistake.

I lost my nerve. "I, uh, I was wondering if you wanted to join us again for dinner?"

The lined hummed for at least thirty seconds. Had he hung up on me?

"Dinner?"

"Yes, Janice—I mean, I would really like you to come." Maybe if I played to his ego, he would accept the invitation. Then, somehow, during dinner I could find a moment to pull him aside and propose a serious meeting. We needed to discuss the divorce and how we were going to make that happen. After today's fiasco, I didn't want to see him alone. Dinner would be the best solution to keep us both out of trouble.

His voice was guarded. "I might be free this evening. Let

me check my schedule."

I could hear him flipping through papers.

"I can be there at eight o'clock." His words were stilted.

"Great."

"Is that all?" he asked. "I'm quite busy here."

"Uh, no, that's it. I'll see you in an hour."

Joaquin gave no response, affirmative or negative, on the other end of the phone.

Dammit, I really messed things up. He sounded less than enthused about meeting us for dinner. Not a good sign.

I wondered what his life had been like up until now. Did he have other lovers? Other women he may have wanted to marry? I might have ruined whatever chance he had for a normal, happy life.

Being away from him all these years, I managed to box up my feelings and set them aside. The less I thought about Joaquin, the less it hurt. And the less it hurt, the easier it was to forget. That included thinking about what my actions did to him. How I may have affected his life. I had been selfish and immature. Deep down, I had known that for awhile now, but had been too much of a wimp to own up to it.

I couldn't be wimpy, however. I had to grow a backbone when it came to Joaquin, and I had to grow it now. No weaknesses could show through anymore.

Maybe if I found out more about what his life had been like after I disappeared, maybe there would be some common ground, something to convince him a divorce would be the best option. To end the hurting now, for both of us, rather than punish each other for a stupid mistake for the rest of our lives.

I looked down at my watch: almost seven thirty. I had no time to change for dinner; Janice and George would be expecting me at Chez México, the nicest restaurant in the hotel. Janice would likely be more than happy to find out Joaquin would be joining us for dinner. She and George would canoodle over their meals, giving me the opportunity to speak to Joaquin.

I headed toward the restaurant located at the southern end of the hotel and shook off my feelings of apprehension.

"Suze, over here!"

Janice and George sat on a padded bench outside the restaurant. She glowed in a shimmery halter top and short, black skirt. She made me feel frumpy in my touristy togs.

I waved.

She sat knee-to-knee with George, their hands clasped together. They looked like honeymooners. Crazy to think these two had only met this morning. Talk about a match made in heaven.

"Hey, good to see you again," said George. "Hope you don't mind me tagging along on your girls' night out."

"Well, Janice isn't the only one bringing a date."

"So you remembered to invite him?" Janice stood up with George and secured the skinny strap of her evening bag on her bare shoulder.

"I told you I would," I said.

Janice touched my arm, "I'm teasing, Suze."

I noticed she wore a lot more make-up than she usually did. Sparkly eye shadow? Glistening lip gloss? What happened to a dash of Chapstick and a few brushes of mascara? And was she wearing my eyeliner?

Wanting to encourage her foray into more girlish behavior than normal, I told her, "You look gorgeous, by the way."

"Uh-uh! Don't change the subject on me." Janice blushed at the compliment. "So, where's your date?" She glanced around the lobby.

"Joaquin's going to be late, and he's not my date."

"So who's this Joaquin guy again?" George asked, looking mighty handsome in khaki pants, a pin-striped shirt, and a navy blazer.

"Oh, he's an old friend of ours," Janice quickly explained. "That's why I booked this hotel. I found out he's the manager. We haven't seen him in ages. He and Suzie used to go out."

"Is that so?"

"Oh, it was nothing. That was such a long time ago." I wanted us to get our table, sit down, and start looking at menus. Anything to get my mind off of Joaquin and what we needed to discuss.

Janice eyed me carefully, "What's wrong with you, Suze? Still green in the gills from kayaking?" She grinned. "Or maybe you need a stiff drink."

"I'm fine. Just a little tired is all. Remember? You got me up before the crack of dawn."

"It was seven o'clock!" She gave George a look that said, *can you believe this girl?*

"I'll have one margarita before dinner. But that's it." I remembered all too well the effect of several margaritas on our first day in Acapulco.

"Yeah, and then you'll have a few shots of tequila, and maybe a Mai Tai," Janice laughed, leading our little threesome to the podium where a tuxedoed maitre d' waited for us.

Some of my uneasiness disappeared around goofy, but lovable, Janice. She had a way of making me feel better in any situation. As we waited for our table, the knot of worry in my stomach loosened a little bit. Maybe a margarita or two would take the edge off my nerves.

It sure couldn't hurt.

*

"When did you say he would get here?" Janice slurred, sipping on her third mixed drink of the night. Empty glasses with teeny umbrellas littered our table. An empty plate that had once held some very tasty appetizers lay bare in the middle of the table.

Where did our waiter go? The clutter bothered me.

"Eight. He said he could be here by eight." I looked at my watch. Eight-thirty. Where was he?

George held up his margarita glass, "To Joaquin, who will

be here by eight."

Janice raised her glass a little too quickly, and some of her drink sloshed over the rim. She didn't seem to notice. "To Joaquin!"

"Did I hear someone calling me?" Joaquin smiled, teeth perfectly aligned, hair tousled yet stylish. He could still take my breath away.

"Have a seat, sweetheart," Janice crowed. She waved her hand at me. "Make room, Suze. He doesn't bite."

We were seated at a large booth, so I slid toward Janice making sure there would be plenty of space between me and Joaquin.

"Thank you." Joaquin unbuttoned his suit jacket. "It seems you haven't ordered yet?" He raised his eyebrows at the un-cleared table. He snapped his fingers and instantly a waiter appeared at his side.

"*Si, señor?*"

In Spanish Joaquin made clear his disapproval of the state of our table. Two busboys appeared out of thin air, whisking away the drink glasses and the empty appetizer plate. Then, he gestured to the waiter to come closer. He whispered in his ear.

"Dinner will be here shortly," he announced with satisfaction, clearly wanting us to be impressed with his authority.

Janice ate it up. Maybe not the admirer he was looking for, but an admirer nonetheless.

"Wow. Hard to believe the last time we saw you, you were a college kid like the rest of us."

Joaquin flashed a smile at her.

I thought George wanted to punch him. Joaquin caused this reaction around other men. He was handsome, flirted with almost any woman, and managed to get his way most of the time. A less secure man than George might have backed down.

George slung his arm possessively around Janice's bare shoulders. She drunkenly leaned into him. "Oh, George! What are people going to think?"

Janice seemed more affected by the alcohol now than she had been ten minutes earlier. I wasn't sure she could make it to the door, much less wait until the entrees arrived.

George must have been thinking the same thing. "Janice? Are you all right?"

Janice leaned forward onto the table, crossed her arms, and rested her head on them. "Mmm-hmmm," she mumbled.

George rubbed her back, "Hey, Janice? Why don't I take you back to your room?"

Take an over-worked lawyer, fly her to Mexico, mix in a few exotic drinks, and voila, you have one wasted girl.

If it weren't George, I might have stood up and insisted I help him. But George? The sweet-as-pie river rafting fool from West Virginia? She couldn't have been safer than if her mother were taking her back up to the suite. He had been treating her like a glass ornament all night long. Besides, I needed a free moment to talk to Joaquin, and sitting in a busy, crowded restaurant was just the place to do it.

Janice mumbled a sleepy assent and threw her arms around George's thick neck. Built like a squished Mac truck, I had no doubts George could carry my skinny little friend if he had to. He pushed her out of the booth, tightly wrapping one arm around her waist, so she didn't slip.

Joaquin told George not to worry about the bill, he would take care of it. We watched as they made their way to the restaurant entrance and out into the lobby. Then, he turned to me. I should have taken the opportunity to slide into George's empty spot on the other side of the table.

He sat so close to me my heart skipped a couple of beats. He made me nervous and self-conscious and horridly aware of the small amount of cleavage peeking out from my v-neck top.

"So, here I am at dinner," he began. "What now?"

I slid one centimeter at a time away from Joaquin and toward the empty bench next to me. I hoped he wouldn't notice.

"We need to talk," I said.

"Yes, we do."

I cleared my throat. "I want a divorce."

His hazel eyes hardened. "No, I don't think so."

"Excuse me?" I grabbed for the glass of ice water in front of me, in desperate need of a drink. My throat felt parched.

"I said no."

Before I could express my outrage, a waiter appeared with a tray laden with food. More food than two people could possibly consume in one sitting. Tacos, flatuas, *ollas* of beans, fajitas, stacks of corn tortillas filled half a dozen plates. The smell of freshly made tortillas and cilantro made my mouth water. Another waiter came in behind the first with a smaller tray bearing a bottle of wine and four wine glasses.

Joaquin directed them to set everything down at our table, snapped his fingers, and then turned to me, "Let's eat."

"Eat? You want me to eat after what you just told me?"

He picked up the opened bottle of wine and poured each of us a glass. "Here, try this. It's from Baja." He nudged the glass my way.

"Give me a divorce, Joaquin." I pushed the glass to the center of the table, and the burgundy wine sloshed out onto the pristine tablecloth.

"I told you, no." He drank deeply of his wine and then set the glass down. He stared at it for a moment, then he turned his attention on me. "You were the one that left me, *querida*."

I shivered at the endearment. In those few words I could hear his humiliation, his anger. I had a hard time thinking about what it must have been like for him after I left. His mother had been completely against our dating. Joaquin knew she would never accept the fact we were in love, that we were serious about one another. Getting married had been the only way to show her.

We both had our reasons for that marriage.

His voice grew louder, "You were my wife, and you left me. And you think I will grant you a divorce with no questions?"

"No," I began in a lowered voice, hoping he would follow suit, "that had never been my intention—to sail in here out of the blue. But I'm only here for a few more days. I don't know when I'll get back to Mexico again. We need to take care of this now."

"What if I don't want a divorce?"

"What?"

"What if I don't want a divorce?" he repeated succinctly.

"Why wouldn't you?" Why in hell would he want to stay married? "I can't imagine you think me a very suitable wife. We've been married twelve years, and we've only spent a few months together. You must have met other women. You must want this as much as I do."

"No. I don't." He scooped up a forkful of food and ate, as if we were discussing the weather.

I couldn't believe it. What in the hell was he doing? "Are you at least going to give me an explanation? Is there no way for me to change your mind?"

"You made me a promise, and then you left me. You made that decision for both of us. Now it's my turn to make a decision. And this is it: No divorce." His eyes bored into mine, and I saw wounded pride reflected in them. He drank some more of his wine.

Now I understood. I had been a blow to his ego. A woman leaving him? It probably seemed impossible to him. I remembered all the women who eyed him, jealous I had been the girl on his arm. Even my roommate, Mercedes, had drooled over him.

"So, you're doing this to punish me, is that it?" My appetite dwindled, and my expression soured. This had not been what I expected. I needed to step back and think about taking a different tack. An amicable divorce was not on the table at this point.

"If that's how you see it. Then, yes." He took another bite of tortilla and beans.

"Then there is no reason for me to stay." I slid away from

him to the opposite edge of the booth. "I hope you enjoy your food."

I walked out of the restaurant, tears burning in my eyes. I would not stay tied to Joaquin for the rest of my life. He couldn't hold on to me forever.

My days in Acapulco were numbered. I would have to do some investigating to find out what might motivate Joaquin to let me go. This couldn't be the way it would end.

Chapter Ten

Returning from the breakfast buffet the next morning, I heard the phone ring through the door of our suite. I rushed inside, dumped my purse on the wingback chair, kicked off my high-heeled shoes, and scooped up the receiver.

"Hello?"

Janice, close behind me, shut the door and gave me a questioning look. I was sure she hoped George was calling.

"Babe? Hey, it's me."

The sound of James's voice in my ear soothed me.

"Sweetie! How are you doing?" I gushed and smiled at Janice so she would know the call was for me. She grinned and disappeared into the bedroom. I heard her turn on the shower.

"I'm fantastic. Guess what?"

"What?" James sounded different—lighter, not as serious as usual.

"I'm going home today," he said, as if he'd told me he'd won the Nobel Prize.

"I thought the conference ended tomorrow." I looked at my watch for the date, being on vacation messed with my mental schedule. I could barely remember the time much less the date. I squinted at the face of my watch. Wednesday.

"It does, but I'm skipping the last session."

I couldn't help but ask, "Why?"

"I asked if I could leave early, and my boss is letting me go."

"Okay." I wondered where the conversation was headed. What wasn't he telling me? "So, you called to tell me that?"

He sighed, sounding aggravated, "Patience, Suze, patience. I'm getting to that."

"All right. I'm all ears." I plopped down on the couch and put my feet up on the coffee table. I noted that my toes could use a new coat of red polish.

"I was thinking back to the argument we had before you left, in the kitchen."

"Uh-huh?"

"I didn't mean to be so pushy, but I thought we could do with a break from each other. Give us some time to think." He paused to rephrase his last statement, "Give *you* time to think."

"And, trust me, I've been doing a lot of that." Little did he know how much of my day was consumed with thinking about him and our future wedding.

"Well, I think we've both done enough thinking."

"And?" I absentmindedly picked at the chipping polish on my right big toe.

"And," I could hear in his voice he was bursting to tell me something, "I bought a ticket down to Acapulco. I'll be there tomorrow afternoon!"

I almost dropped the phone on the floor. "What?" My fingers stopped in mid-pick, my toe half red, half flesh-colored.

"I knew you'd be surprised!"

James was so predictable, so *not* spontaneous. In the last few weeks I'd watched a different James emerge. What happened to the man who couldn't complain at a restaurant even if his food arrived at the table cold, burned, and nowhere near what he'd ordered? It took a lot to push him over the edge, to make him move out of his comfort zone. Flying to Acapulco on a romantic whim definitely was out of his comfort zone.

And leaving a tech convention so he could make this big romantic gesture? What had he been smoking?

"Goodness. Are you really coming down?"

"You have six more days left down there. Why not have some fun ourselves? Janice isn't the only one that needs a vacation."

I liked this new, improved James. I made the rash decisions in this relationship. It was nice to have James take that role for a change.

"And you said she met some guy down there?" he asked. "I'm sure she'd be more than happy to have me around to occupy your time."

I smiled, imagining James and me romping in the surf, sleeping in late, eating breakfast in bed. "But we'd have to book another room."

"I've already made the arrangements."

"Sounds perfect." Then my fantasies of a pre-honeymoon with James were cut short. How would I keep my hunt for a divorce a secret if he were here with me? How would I find time to slip away? And, God help me, how would I keep James from running into Joaquin? My stomach fluttered.

"Yep. I can hardly wait to see you at the airport."

"Airport?" My worries built slowly, but I couldn't let James hear anything but eagerness in my voice. "Yes, I'll be at the airport. When's your flight arriving?"

I wrote down the pertinent information on a piece of hotel stationery I found in a desk drawer in the living room. His plane would be landing at three tomorrow afternoon. A little over twenty-four hours from now. I tried not to panic.

I sent a kiss to him over the phone line and hung up.

My feelings were mixed—although excited James would be here with me tomorrow, I feared my plans would be revealed. I needed to work on Joaquin today, if possible. Find out why he was so eager to stay married. It didn't make sense.

I had one day to get my act together. But where to begin?

Janice flew out of the bedroom, her short hair clipped into

hot rollers. "So, what's new with James?"

It took me a minute to find my voice. I had never seen Janice do more than finger-comb her short hair after a shower—her idea of 'styling.' Where did these rollers come from? It was remarkable how much of an effect George had on Janice's personal grooming habits after only a few days together.

"He's coming to Acapulco."

"What? Are you serious?" Janice took a seat next to me on the couch to get the scoop. "That's great!"

"Really? I thought maybe you'd be upset he would intrude on our little girl power adventure."

Janice unclipped the round rollers from her hair, setting them one at a time on the coffee table next to my feet. Fluffy curls of light brown hair stuck out around her head like a dandelion gone to seed. Maybe the grooming habits hadn't been perfected quite yet.

"Nah, that's okay," she said "You know I absolutely adore James."

(True. She did. Whenever James and I traveled up north to visit my mom, Janice inevitably ended up on my mother's doorstep with a bottle of wine, a bouquet of flowers, and once, even a tray of deli meats from the grocery store. From that first visit home with James to the last visit less than six months ago, Janice had been a fixture at my mom's. Her own parents had retired and traveled the country in their RV, so my mom had become Janice's replacement parent.

Janice had approved of James right away, noting his well-dressed exterior and chivalrous attentions. She had also declared that he was a "hottie that didn't even know it, and those were the best kind to have.")

"I'm so glad you feel that way. He also booked us another room—but I'll stay here if you want. James would understand."

"Don't be silly, Suze!" She slapped me on the arm, one final roller slipping from her short hair. "I could use some time—alone." A blush crept up the side of her neck and flooded her cheeks.

"Why, Janice!" I said with an expression of mock shock on my face, "I didn't know I was cramping your style."

"Quit it." She jabbed me in the side with her bony elbow. The last curler fell from her hair into her lap, and she clutched it in her hand, smoothing her fingers over its bumpy surface. "George is just so wonderful—"

I knew she couldn't stand up to much more ribbing, so I eased off. "I know, hon, I know."

We sat there for a moment, reflecting on the respective men in our lives.

I had a hot flash of muddled emotions. On the one hand, I couldn't wait to share Mexico with James, to go exploring down the beaches, shopping in the markets, relaxing by the pool. But on the other hand, I was terrified he would figure out my secret and run into Joaquin. I tried to put it out of my mind and concentrate instead on what I could accomplish before he got here. Or, at least, what I hoped to accomplish.

Janice broke the comfortable silence first. "Well, I need to finish getting ready." She stood up and headed for her suitcase.

"Yeah, I've been meaning to ask you, what are you getting ready for?"

"Oh, didn't I tell you?" She slipped on a pair of square-heeled shoes. "George and I signed up for salsa lessons."

"Salsa lessons? Since when have you been interested in dancing?" Janice might be athletic, but she was not graceful.

She gave me a hurt little frown. "George suggested it—and we're in Mexico. What better place to learn?"

"I'm sorry, Janice, I didn't mean it to sound like that. I was just surprised is all."

Her frown straightened some. "I know it's not quite my thing, but we have that big party tomorrow, and I'm sure there'll be a chance to dance."

God, the party. James would be here while the hotel hosted their Welcome Fiesta. Joaquin was sure to attend. How would I keep them apart? Panic roared to life inside my head. I would have to stay with James in the hotel room all night. He wouldn't protest that idea. Right?

"Well, have a good time. Don't let me stop you." I hoped I kept the fear out of my voice as I shooed her toward the door.

She tripped awkwardly through the room, trying to imitate a ballerina en pointe, her arms circled in an 'O' above her head. I giggled at her lanky body, more like Olive Oyl than Cyd Charisse.

"You'll be wishing you took some lessons come tomorrow night," she warned. She glided out into the hall, and I got up from the couch to shut the door behind her.

Now for my afternoon plans.

*

I opened the door marked *Director General* and entered a small ante-room. An older woman in a form-fitting navy suit sat behind a desk, talking on the phone in Spanish so quickly I could barely catch more than a word or two. Behind her desk I noticed another door—Joaquin's office, I assumed.

"*Perdóname*," I began. From the words I could distinguish, it sounded as if she were making a personal call.

Still talking on the phone, the secretary watched me with her heavily made-up eyes. She didn't seem to be in any hurry to end her conversation. Feeling self-conscious, I sat down in one of the chairs by her desk.

After several more minutes of chatter, the woman hung up and glared at me.

"*Cómo le ayudo a usted?*"

"I want to see Mr. Hernandez, please."

"And you are?" she asked, her accent heavy on her tongue.

"Suzette Eisenhart. An old friend. He knows I'm staying here."

After hearing my relationship to her boss, a hard edge glinted in her stare. She sized me up, judging me. I couldn't help but squirm under her scrutiny. Who did this woman think she was?

"Mr. Hernandez is not available right now." She tugged the skirt of her suit down over her knees and swept away invisible dust off of her pristine desk. I had the feeling she wished she could sweep me away as easily.

"If he's here, I need to see him."

"I told you, miss, he is not available."

"I am always available for my friends, Celia." Joaquin stood in the door behind the secretary's desk, his shirtsleeves rolled up to the elbow, tie loosened. He wore navy trousers and a yellow-and-blue tie. Handsome as the devil, and he knew it.

Celia watched me with a penetrating gaze. "Of course, señor," she said with a happy lilt to her voice, as if she had been nothing but friendly and cordial to me the entire time.

What did I do to this woman to have her despise me so much? Wear the wrong perfume?

Joaquin invited me into his office, and I swept past him. The secretary sniffed as I went by. I was glad Joaquin's treatment of me annoyed her.

Joaquin had a spacious office filled with leather and mahogany furniture. A beautiful white orchid graced a small table near the window—a feminine touch that seemed out of place in the very masculine room.

Must have been a gift. Maybe from his secretary. Or a female admirer.

I banished that thought from my head. I shouldn't be bothered by the thought of Joaquin having other women in his life.

He shut the door behind me.

He leaned against the edge of his desk. I could feel his gaze sliding over my figure. "To what do I owe this pleasure?" He buttoned up his shirt and tightened his tie. Back to being the Hotel Manager, it seemed.

"I'm sure you don't need to ask." I took a seat in one of the straight-backed leather chairs. "I'm here to discuss our divorce."

"I already told you, Suzie, I don't want a divorce."

"I know, but that's not acceptable to me. There must be a way for us to work this out." I crossed my legs carefully, prudishly to show him how my feelings had changed toward him. "There had never been any marriage. And I'm not in love with you anymore. What more do you want from me?"

He continued to lean against his desk, folding his arms across the broad expanse of his chest. "Why should I do this for you," he lifted an eyebrow, "when you have done so little for me?"

I looked up at him from the comfortable black leather chair. Trying to discern what he wanted me to say. What could he possibly want from me? Money? He seemed to be doing very well for himself. I looked around the room, taking in the award plaques and expensive furnishings.

I noticed several framed photographs that hung on the wall behind his desk.

"Who is that?" I pointed at the largest picture hanging directly behind him, curiosity guiding me—a photo of a girl, about eleven or twelve. She stood in front of a massive bougainvillea that crawled over a garden arch, its bright pink blooms a sea of color. I stood up and moved toward the picture, wanting to get a closer look at the child.

Before he could answer me, I knew who this child was. The wide-set hazel eyes were identical to Joaquin's.

He stood silent behind me.

I turned. "This is your child?"

"Yes, that is my daughter," he said without any pride or emotion in his voice.

I couldn't think. Although it made sense Joaquin would have been involved with other women after I had gone, to be confronted with the evidence left my chest feeling hollow.

He has a daughter.

"Are you so surprised, Suzie?" He moved toward me, buttoning the final button on his shirt cuff. "Did you think I would wait for you forever?"

I was confused. This made no sense. If he moved on with his life after I left, why did we almost end up having sex in my room yesterday? Why was he so angry at me for disappearing? Asking for a divorce should be a relief for us both.

He stepped closer, to within a foot of me. I could feel his body heat. I pulled back.

"No, I never thought that." I glanced at the other photos looking for someone he had yet to mention, "And her mother?"

"We were old friends. After you left, she had been happy enough to console me."

For some reason, this thought sickened me. Yes, I went home and never contacted Joaquin. But I had been miserable and heart-broken. I had no one back home I could confide in, not even my own mother. Months passed before I had been able to get over both my father's death and the loss of Joaquin.

Now, it sounded as if he'd jumped right into a relationship with another woman the minute I stepped foot out of Mexico. I shouldn't care so much about something that happened so long ago, but I did. It felt betrayed. It made all the worrying and suffering I had gone through over the last decade seem so pointless. I could have asked for a divorce years ago and saved myself so much heartache.

"And you're still with her now?" I found myself asking. Why should I care? I gave up my rights to care about him twelve years ago.

Twelve years.

I picked up another small, framed photo on his desk of a birthday party. His daughter was smiling, standing in front of a huge birthday cake. Above her head stretched a banner: "*Feliz Cumpleaños, Ariana!*" Underneath was the date, *agosto 29.*

I felt Joaquin's gaze on me.

"So, are you enjoying your stay here?" he asked.

I set the picture back on the desk. "I didn't come here to have a vacation. I came here for one reason only: to get a divorce." I backed away from the photos. "Friday, I have an appointment with a lawyer in town. You're going to be there with me." I sounded more confident than I felt.

"Am I?" Joaquin took a seat behind his large mahogany desk.

"I'll be here at nine a.m. sharp, and we can go together."

His eyes were hard and unyielding, his mouth a grim line. He stared at me for a moment, thinking. Then, his features softened.

I took a step back. I thought he would reach for me, pull me to him again, like that day in the hotel room.

"Maybe there is something I want, too."

I flinched. "Oh?"

I had been expecting this. Of course he wanted something from me. He wasn't still in love with me. The scene in the hotel room from the other day had been a show. He wanted me here, begging him for a divorce. I had played right into his little trap, hadn't I?

"Yes, and you'll do it, too, if you want this divorce so badly."

"What is it?" I was afraid to hear the answer.

"I need you to play wife for one night." He let that sink in for a moment. Maybe testing to see how I would react. "Tomorrow. At the party."

"What party?"

"The Welcome Fiesta."

Where Janice hoped she could show off her new salsa moves. The same night James would be arriving in Acapulco. "I–I don't know–why would you want me to?"

"No questions," he snapped. "You want a divorce, yes?"

I nodded.

"Then, you will be my wife for one evening. The next day, I will sign whatever papers you want."

"Really?"

"Yes."

"How long do I have to pretend to be your wife?"

"Pretend, Susie? You are my wife, or none of this would be necessary, would it?"

The humiliation was almost too much to bear.

"Near the end of the fiesta," he explained, "when most of the guests have gone up to their rooms, I want you next to me, as if we are lovers."

I felt my face turn warm at the thought. "And that's it?"

"That's it. I will take care of everything else."

I was so eager to take this chance I didn't even care to ask what or who this display would be for. One night, for a few minutes, I could pretend to be in love with Joaquin. Couldn't I? I could find away to send James away—maybe get Janice to distract him. I would figure it out.

"All right," I said. "If that is the only way."

"You understand, it must be believable."

"Yes," I said, "I understand." Maybe he wanted to make another woman jealous? The mother of his son? Someone else? Did it really matter?

I would do anything he wanted to get his signature on those divorce papers. By Friday, my troubles would be over. My worries gone. James and I could go forward with our wedding. I felt free for the first time in years.

Chapter Eleven

"So are you excited?" Janice asked me, spinning across the floor of our suite on her toothpick legs. Muscular toothpicks, but toothpicks nonetheless.

"Yes, I can't believe he's actually coming."

"Oh, what a man in love won't do for his girl," said Janice.

James would be here in a few hours, and I felt positively giddy inside. We'd only been apart for a few days, but it felt as if I hadn't seen him in months. Being in a foreign country will do that to you, I guess. Make you feel different. Give you a different perspective on things.

I was out of my element. In a different routine. Eating foreign food and drinking margaritas every night. A far cry from James's meatloaf and my homemade garlic mashed potatoes.

Today was the first day I really missed our morning trip to Starbucks for our daily shot of caffeine: me, a latte with a shot of hazelnut, him, a tall cup of black coffee, French Roast.

"It'll be fun with him here at the party tonight. Me and George, you and James. A real double date!" Janice stopped twirling and sat down dizzily on the couch, a huge smile on her face. She ran her hands through her hair and shook her head, making her hair stick out wildly from her head. "This is probably the best vacation I will ever have."

"You and George are really hitting it off, aren't you?" I took another bite of my eggs. We were spoiling ourselves with room service.

"Isn't he wonderful?" She got up from the couch and started practicing her salsa steps again.

"Janice, you need to calm down or you'll be too tired to move much less dance." She had flitted about the suite all morning.

We'd decided to turn most of the day into a Pamper Party—brunch in the room, self-manicuring and pedicuring, in-room massages. James would be at the airport at three, George would pick Janice up at five, and we would all meet by the pool for the Welcome Fiesta at seven. So we wanted some time together being girly before we had to get the guys.

Not that Janice was particularly girly, but George brought out her long-hidden feminine side. A side I didn't even know existed. She wore more make-up than I did at the moment. Maybe a little too much eye shadow and a too-bright lipstick color, but I wasn't about to point out small things like that to a woman who only just discovered the joys of Maybelline.

"I can't help it," she said. "I don't want to stop moving. I had no idea salsa could be so much fun." A few more twirls, and then she bumped into a lamp table, knocking it over. "Whoops!"

Her usual gangly awkwardness reappeared. The clock had struck midnight and Cinderella was back in rags.

"Careful." I got up from the couch, cotton balls between my freshly-painted toes, and waddled over to the table to right it.

"Sorry," Janice said sheepishly. She sat down next to her half-eaten plate of food. "Guess there'll be enough time tonight to do some dancing."

"Exactly.

The phone rang, and I made my way across the room to

pick it up. A couple of cotton balls fell out of my toes' grip, and I swore under my breath. Nothing worse than smearing a freshly painted toe.

"Hello?"

"Hey, honey, it's me."

"James!" I sat down on the nearest chair and started tugging the cotton from between my toes, the phone tucked under my chin. "I thought you'd be at the airport waiting in line by now."

"I am. I wanted to call you one last time before I had to turn off my cell phone."

My heart swelled at his sweetness. He always did little things like this. Bringing flowers home. Making me potato salad and barbecue chicken, my favorite meal, on a really bad day. Folding my laundry into neat little piles when I had a big project at work to finish and worked lots of extra hours. He did much better laundry than I did.

"I'll be waiting at the airport for you. Okay?"

"I can hardly wait. I love you, Suze."

"I love you, too."

The phone clicked in my ear. James would be shutting his cell phone off now as he waited outside the gate for his plane. I looked at my watch. Eleven o'clock. Just a few more hours, and he would be here with me. The beach, the sun, his hand in mine.

I tried hard not to think about later this evening. When I would have to find some excuse to leave him alone for an hour or so to play wife to Joaquin. It was easier not to think about it. To play it by ear when the time came. I would figure out a way.

"Aw, you guys are too cute." Janice munched on a croissant.

I rolled my eyes at her. James and I were in love and engaged to be married, but we were never one of those couples to talk baby talk or to hang all over each other in public. We held hands, we gave each other quick kisses on the lips, but never full make-out sessions in front of friends and neighbors.

So this little window into our love life was a tad uncomfortable for me.

I changed the subject, "Aren't you going kayaking with George in an hour or so?"

"Yep. George and his friends will be here at one." She took a swig of water out of her water bottle. "That's okay with you, right? I feel bad leaving you alone in the room."

George came to Acapulco with a couple of buddies from his white water rafting group, and they wanted to meet the mysterious Janice. She agreed yesterday to a group kayaking excursion. I, of course, had been more than willing to pass on the opportunity to publicly humiliate myself in a foreign country. Plus, I wanted to give Janice more time alone with George.

"It's fine, Janice, really. Vacations for me mean a lot of lazing around, eating, and reading. I've got the first two down." I scooped up another bite of eggs to prove it. "And now all I need is a couple of hours to make a dent in one of the books I brought along with me." I held up the thick paperback on the couch next to me to emphasize the point.

"If you're sure—"

"I'm sure."

"And there's nothing I can say to convince you to come along?"

"Nothing." I took a sip of coffee. "But I want you to promise me that you'll give me all the details on George's friends. I'm so curious."

"I am, too." Janice tore off another chunk of her croissant. Only that woman could eat two croissants slathered in butter and not worry about where the calories were going. "They've been in this rafting club for years. Since they got out of college, I think."

"Is that when George started his company?" George owned and operated the second largest rafting tour company in West Virginia, Adventure Rafting Tours, I think it was called.

"Yeah. He and Nick—that's one of the guys he's here with."

"Nervous?"

"A little."

"Well, don't be. You look fantastic." Janice could clean up and be quite beautiful when she wanted to. She finally seemed comfortable in her own skin. Her face glowed, even with the too-dark eye shadow and wrong shade of lip gloss. She had dressed her lean body more feminine than usual with a pair of hip-hugging shorts and a strappy top with a row of sequins across the neckline. I actually felt frumpy next to her. A first.

"Oh, Suze." She blushed. She still hadn't learned how to take a compliment.

"You're welcome." I looked at my watch. "He should be here any minute."

As soon as the words were out of my mouth, someone politely rapped on our door. I jumped up, wanting to give Janice a moment to collect herself.

"George!" He was the kind of guy who made you want to smile the minute you see him and give him a hug. A sweet, honest man who probably never said a bad word about anyone. "Come on in."

"Thanks," George ambled his way into our suite. He caught sight of Janice and let out a low whistle. "Hey, Gorgeous."

Janice blushed from her toes to her ears. "Hi."

I tried to bow out gracefully. "Well, I need to go take a shower. I'll leave you two guys alone." I edged toward the bedroom door.

I don't think they even heard me. I witnessed a close embrace, a passionate kiss, and then I ducked inside the bedroom, shutting the door behind me.

I sat on the bed for a moment. Seeing Janice and George together, I thought of James. He would be waiting for me at the airport in a few hours. I didn't deserve such a great guy. James had never been anything but honest, supportive, and loving since we started dating.

I wish I could say the same.

But I would fix it. It would all be over soon.

*

"Flight 265 from San Antonio now arriving at Gate 26," the crackly voice over the loudspeaker announced, repeating the same message in Spanish. James's flight. He would be here in front of me in a few minutes.

I had left the hotel with my head spinning, ready to put my plan into motion. Well, it wasn't much of a plan. I had never been very good about those kinds of things. I liked to think more on my feet, make spontaneous decisions. My marriage to Joaquin was evidence of that.

The party started at seven. Joaquin and I had agreed to meet around eleven. He promised it wouldn't take more than an hour to play my little role. An hour. I had to find a reason to be gone an hour.

I stood near the gate marked "*Venidas*/Arrivals." A flood of people rushed past me.

"Suzie? Hey, over here."

I had been so caught up in my own thoughts, I didn't even notice James had gotten off the plane. He appeared taller and thinner than I remembered. But his eyes were the same cool forest green. A field of calm amid the chaos.

"Oh, honey, I'm sorry." I reached out to give him a quick hug and a kiss, glad to have his familiar warmth next to me again. "I was kinda zoned out there. How was your flight?"

"Something wrong?" He swung an arm across my shoulders and pulled me close.

I looked at him, even on vacation James dressed as if he were going to work: khaki pants, short-sleeved golf shirt tucked in neatly, loafers. The only way you could tell he was a tourist was the pair of sunglasses propped up on top of his head and the set of golf clubs he dragged behind him.

"Golf clubs?" I didn't recall us having a discussion about the fine golf courses of Acapulco.

"I thought maybe you'd want to do some girl stuff with Janice."

"And that you could find a few hours to practice your swing?"

"Obviously, you didn't realize, but Playa Del Mexico has an excellent nine hole course," he said, smiling. "Right on the beach."

"I see. Been doing your research, huh?" I poked him in the ribs with my elbow.

"You take your vacation your way, and I'll take mine my way." He gave my shoulder a squeeze.

I loved his smell. A little bit of aftershave mixed with Irish Spring.

All my worries dissipated with a hug from the man I loved. I was safe, comfortable. Any stray thoughts about the evening ahead I purged from my mind. It would be an unpleasant task to play Joaquin's wife, but it would guarantee me what I wanted, and I wasn't going to spoil this time with James by thinking about it.

"So, where's the rest of your luggage? Or is this all you need when you travel?" I gestured at his golf bag.

"If I could fit my toothbrush and a change of underwear in there, you know that would be the case." He kissed the top of my head.

I laughed. He could be as much as a goof as I could be sometimes. A good quality in a man. Not one that they really mention in any of those dating books. Goofy and a bit on the nerdy side? My ideal man. Well, of course he had to look good in a pair of khaki shorts. That didn't hurt things.

When we headed toward baggage claim, I made sure to get a quick look at James's backside. I smiled to myself, because he had no idea how cute he looked, how scrumptious. If we weren't in a crowd of strangers, I probably would have goosed him. Yes, I had really missed him the few days I had been away.

"So, what's this about some party tonight?"

"It's a fiesta," I said. "You know, mariachis and margaritas?"

"Okay, so it's a fiesta," he corrected. "Is that where I get to meet this George character?"

"You'll like George."

"Is that so?"

"Yes, that is so. You'll see. They're like Bogey and Bacall. Rogers and Astaire."

"James and Suzette?"

"James and Suzette."

He smiled. Both of us ignored the luggage filing past us on the conveyor belt. He had arrived, and that was all that mattered to me.

Chapter Twelve

"Where have you been?"

I sat by myself in an almost-empty university cafeteria. A plate of half-eaten French fries and an open text book were on the table in front of me when Janice sat down.

"Around." I picked at my fries and tried to concentrate on the reading assignment I should have finished days ago.

"You know we have a field trip tomorrow, right?" She took one of my fries and dipped it in the splotch of ketchup on my plate.

That girl could eat French fries until her eyes fell out and would never gain an ounce.

"Yeah, I know. Six a.m. at the school entrance." I rubbed my eyes. It was after ten o'clock already, and I wanted to finish the last ten pages of reading before I went to bed.

Once a month our professor-in-residence from Vincent College scheduled a weekend field trip for all the study-abroad students to various places of interest within a few hours' drive of Puebla. Professor Burnham, an aging art history professor, was the current teacher-in-residence. The class was a required part of our study while enrolled at the university.

This weekend we were off to Teotihuacán, the famous

Aztec pyramids right outside of Mexico City. The pyramids were the most touristy destination we would be visiting the whole school year, and I wasn't looking forward to spending the day dodging tourists and the Mexican street vendors hawking their souvenirs.

"You wanna come back to the dorm with me? Chill for a bit? Maybe watch some TV?" She sounded lonely and a bit forlorn.

"I really have to finish this reading first." I stuck my nose deep in my book, hoping to give her the hint to leave me alone. "I have to get caught up on all my homework."

She tipped the top edge of my book down, forcing me to look her in the eye. "Maybe you should try staying on campus one of these weekends. I mean, do you have to spend every single waking hour either talking about Joaquin or taking the bus to meet up with Joaquin?" Letting go of my book, she snagged another fry off my plate.

"Why don't you get some of your own fries?"

"Kitchen's closed." She took a big bite of French fry. "You didn't answer my question."

"I can keep up with my assignments."

"Then why are you here half-asleep trying to read sixteenth century poetry?"

I closed my book, pushed it to one side. "What's up with you?" The annoyance in my voice echoed through the quiet cafeteria.

"What's up with *me*?" She lowered her voice to an irritated whisper. "You're the one who's got issues. What exactly is going on with you guys, anyway? You've been attached at the hip since October. We signed up for this so we could do something adventurous, meet new people, get some culture."

"That was why *you* decided to sign up."

A hurt look crossed Janice's face. "I thought we were going to do this together. I thought—"

"Well, you thought wrong." I shoved my books to the side. "I can't help it if I met Joaquin. I can't help what I feel for him."

"What *do* you feel for him, Suze?"

Janice looked me right in the eye, waiting for the truth, and I couldn't give it to her. I couldn't own up to the seriousness of my relationship. What was I so scared of, anyway? That she would tell someone? That she would take it away from me somehow?

I wimped out. "I don't know, Janice. We have a good time together. And my Spanish has gotten so much better being around him all the time. He's my own personal tutor."

"Your own tutor?"

"Yeah." Once the lies started coming, I couldn't stop. "Joaquin's great and all, but, face it, we're going home in May. Back to the States. Back to Vincent. Joaquin's a lot of fun."

"And he's gorgeous."

"Yeah, that doesn't hurt any. What's wrong with having a little fling?"

"I wish we could spend more time together. Just you and me. I miss you, Suze."

I pushed my half-empty plate of fries right under her nose as a peace offering. "How about this? On the field trip this weekend, it's just you and me. No boys. And no talking about boys. We'll do whatever you want."

"Really?" Her face beamed, and she swiped a few fries off of the offered plate.

"Really."

"Well, then, let's try to hike the pyramids—all the way to the top!" She said this as if she were discussing reaching the summit of Mount Everest, a French fry aloft in her hand like the Statue of Liberty holding her torch.

"Do you have any idea how high those things are? Did you read any of the materials from Professor Burnham? They're ancient Stairmasters."

"Oh, they aren't *that* high." This, coming from Janice, the woman built to run super-marathons. She took a bite of her torch-fry. "Anyway, it would be good for us. All that climbing. And think of the pictures we could take from up there."

"Yeah, of all the smog over the city. Sounds lovely."

This time Janice reached out for my soda and took a sip, "Suzie, you promised we could do whatever I want, remember? When are you ever going to get this chance again?"

I thought about what she'd said, but she had no idea why that question made me pause. Joaquin and I only had a few months left to spend with together before I had to go back home. I didn't want to contemplate leaving in May. I pushed it as far to the back of my mind as I could.

"Will you take my picture for me on top of the Pyramid of the Sun?"

I took the last French fry from the plate. "You betcha."

*

"I'll see you tomorrow morning?" I asked Janice as we stepped into the guard shack separating the girls' dormitory from the rest of campus. It was an armed fortress with high brick walls sporting ironwork spikes all along the top. The only way in and out of the girls' dormitory and the courtyard surrounding it was through the guard shack.

"Bright and early." Janice winked at me and hurried past the guard's desk to the courtyard door.

I yawned at the thought. Midnight approached and our bus left campus at seven in the morning. As I crossed through the guard shack, a piece of white paper on the bulletin board caught my eye. "Sra. Eisenhart" had been scribbled on it in red marker.

"*Señorita* Eisenhart?" I said to the guard sitting behind the counter, pointing at the piece of paper behind him.

He spun his chair around, snatched the paper off the board, and dropped it on the counter. Guess someone was unhappy he'd pulled a Friday night shift.

"Gracias." I unfolded the note - a phone message from Joaquin.

Llámame. Te quiero.

He wanted me to call him. The time on the note indicated he had called a couple of hours earlier.

I held it to my lips, thinking.

A bank of phones sat on the counter by the guard. I set the note on the counter, picked up a receiver, and dialed Joaquin's number.

One ring, and then "*Bueno?*"

I'd recognize that deep, sexy voice anywhere.

"It's me, Joaquin."

"*Querida. Mi bonita,* Suzie."

"I miss you. It was nice to see your note waiting for me when I came in."

"Where have you been?"

"Studying."

"I wish you were here with me in the city. Do you have to go on that trip tomorrow?"

"It's required as part of the program."

"Where are you they taking you?"

"Teotihuacán."

"You're going to the pyramids?"

"Yeah. All day." I fiddled with the note on the counter in front of me, folding and refolding it. *Te quiero.* He loved me.

"I could meet you there."

"What?" I dropped the note.

"I could meet you there. Don't you want to see me?"

"Of course I do, but—"

"Then, say you'll meet me. We could spend the whole day there together."

"But Joaquin, the rest of my group." I thought of Janice and the plans we'd made that evening.

"You could sneak away."

"I couldn't."

"Yes, you could. No one would notice."

"Janice would." More likely she would be crushed if I sneaked off to be with Joaquin.

"She is your friend, no? She wouldn't say anything. I want

115

to see you."

"Joaquin." My insides quivered at the idea of being next to him, up close against his body.

"I have to see you, *querida*. Please." The urgency in his voice caused me to pause.

He needed me. He wanted me.

"I guess I'll think of something." I closed my eyes and the guilt kicked in the minute I said it. How could I do that to Janice? But I didn't even try to take back the words. I thought about my friend for a few short seconds, and then her image disappeared. I could see her any time. We could find another day to do something together.

"Meet me near the Visitor's Center."

"All right. At nine?"

"Nine o'clock. I'll be there."

"Good night."

"*Te quiero.*"

"*Te quiero, también.*"

I'd made a promise to Janice not an hour ago, and already I was breaking it. The social, pretty college girl was dumping the shy, bookish friend for the chance to spend time with a good-looking guy. The thought seemed cruel, like the plot to a bad teenage TV drama.

She'll understand. That's what I kept telling myself all the way back to the dorm. *She'll understand.*

*

The first rays of the morning sun filtered through the blinds covering my dorm room window. I could barely open my eyes. Too early to be up on a Saturday.

"Suzie?" Mercedes, my roommate, still lay in her bed.

"Yeah?" I checked my pack for my water bottle and trip notebook.

"Your *novio* called last night." Her voice was bitter. She had never reconciled the fact that Joaquin had fallen for me

116

instead of her.

"I know. I got his message. Any others you got stashed away in there?" I pointed at her locked closet.

She aggravated me lately. Several times, she had pulled messages from Joaquin off the notice board and hid them. I'm not sure if she was jealous or just disliked me, but every now and again I found notes torn to pieces in the bottom of her closet. But I had no one to complain to. The guard down at the entrance had no obligation to make sure I got my messages.

But most roommates weren't conniving little bitches either.

She gave me a disdainful look and then sat up in bed, her beautiful thick hair looking better than it had any right to at seven a.m. on a Saturday morning.

"He called me, too, you know," she said sweetly, twisting a strand of her long, dark hair. "I told him there were plenty of other boys on the tour tomorrow who could watch out for you."

I narrowed my eyes. "Why would Joaquin call you?"

"You don't believe me?" She stopped twirling her hair. "He's my friend, remember? I knew him well before you ever met him."

"He's not your friend anymore." I zipped my backpack closed. "You're a liar. He never called you."

"What if I told you that Joaquin was in love with me?" She smoothed the blanket around her legs. "And not with you."

"You're crazy, Mercedes." This girl had no shame. What would she tell me next? That they were running off to Vegas together? "You might have had a crush on him in high school, but that's it. He told me all about it. You two were barely even friends." I straightened the sheets on my bed.

"Is that what he told you?" Her voice cracked.

I looked up at her and thought I saw something in her eyes for a moment, but then they hardened into brown pebbles.

"He's a liar," she said. "Ask him."

I sighed in irritation.

"You ask him," she insisted.

"As if I care what you believe. Joaquin can barely even tolerate you." I fluffed my pillow with a little more energy than needed. "And you tell me he's in love with you? God, how sad, Mercedes." I grabbed my backpack and stepped out of our room, slamming the door behind me.

"You ask him, Suzie! He loves *me*," Mercedes's muffled voice called out.

What a freak. She had been nothing but trouble since Joaquin and I started dating. He only had eyes for me, and she couldn't stand it.

After a few missed phone calls and a bouquet of red roses that 'accidentally' ended up in the trash, Joaquin and I both learned that relying on Mercedes for anything was impossible. And now she believed Joaquin was in love with her? Would it ever stop? How ridiculous.

Exiting the suite, I tried to push Mercedes and her manipulations out of my head.

Chapter Thirteen

"James!" exclaimed Janice. Her cheeks were sunburned and the stripe of zinc oxide down her nose had smeared, exposing the pointy tip. "You're here!"

She rushed forward into the suite to give him a quick hug.

"Hey, Janice," he hugged her back and gave her a wry grin. "Good to see you."

"How was the kayaking?" I packed the last of my belongings in my suitcase. James and I were staying in a suite on another floor.

"Fantastic." Catching sight of herself in a mirror over the refrigerator, she wiped at the zinc oxide with her towel. "You really should have come along."

James gave me a questioning look over Janice's spiky hair.

"Yes, I took the sea kayaking course, too," I said, answering his unspoken question. "If you can believe it."

Janice dropped her towel on the back of the couch, wrapped an arm around my shoulders, and squeezed, "And our girl was marvelous, I tell you. Like a fish takes to water."

"More like a fish out of water," I said with a smile. "And, besides, Janice, you knew I had to pick up James. No way could I have taken that trip with you and made it back in time."

"I suppose so."

"Well, there's still time left to try out your new skills. Maybe while I'm out on the golf course," James said.

"Of course. You would never leave without those clubs, would you?" asked Janice.

"Not on your life, missy."

"Would someone help me please?" I managed to shove all of my clothes, shoes, and toiletries back into my suitcase, but I couldn't get the zipper to close all the way. An unsightly bulge stuck out on one side, making it look as if it had swallowed a basketball.

"Man to the rescue." James rushed to my side with a playful smile on his face. He examined my huge suitcase carefully, looking at it from all sides. "I think I see the problem here." He reached inside the half-zipped bag and pulled out half a dozen pairs of shoes. "Voila!" He zipped it closed in triumph.

"And what am I supposed to do with all of my shoes?" I nodded my head at the sad little pile on the floor.

James grabbed the ice bucket off the top of the mini refrigerator. "How about putting them in here?" He tossed the shoes into the empty bucket.

"In an ice bucket?"

"Just until we get to the room." Grabbing the last pair, he turned to Janice, "You don't mind, do you?"

"Nah, go ahead. Bring it back whenever." She shooed us out the door. James dragged my heavy suitcase on wheels, and I carried an ice bucket stuffed with flats, sandals, and pumps.

"We'll see you later tonight" James waved with his free hand.

"Out by the pool, right?" Janice asked me.

"Yep. By the pool at seven."

Out in the hall, I pressed the elevator button to go up. We were one floor above Janice. Somehow, James managed to get us an ocean-front room as well.

The doors slid open, and I followed behind him, giving

him plenty of space to position my large suitcase.

"Which floor?" asked a familiar voice.

I looked up to see Joaquin. His face was a blank, but his eyes were cold as ice water. I turned hot and cold, unable to answer. Of all the elevators in the hotel, why did we have to catch this one?

James said, "Fourteen, please."

I turned my back to Joaquin and closed my eyes, trying to control the panic coursing through my body. James would know something was wrong. He might guess that—

The door slid open. Our short trip to the next floor was mercifully over.

"Hon," James urged. "The door's open. Let's not hold the elevator."

My muscles thawed. My feet moved. Joaquin stood so close to me in the cramped elevator that when I exited, my arm brushed against his sleeve.

I shivered.

James grasped my elbow and pulled me the rest of the way out of the elevator. As the doors were about to close, Joaquin reached out his hand to hold them open.

I braced myself for it, the confrontation, the revealing of information James had no idea was coming. I felt sick.

"You dropped your shoe, *querida.*" Joaquin held out a red strappy heel. One of a pair I planned on wearing that evening.

I'm sure I flamed as red as my shoe at the endearment.

Gingerly, I took the heel from his outstretched hand and squeaked out a thank you. Dumping the shoe unceremoniously into the ice bucket with the rest of my footwear, I turned away from the elevator doors. I couldn't look at him. Not with James here.

The doors whooshed shut.

I let out the breath I had been holding.

"What does '*querida*' mean?" James asked. His eyes scanned my face, which was probably still flushed pink.

"Oh, I guess he was flirting with me." I hoped he would

believe me. Thank goodness James hardly knew a word of Spanish.

"It was almost as if he knew you."

"Hmmm," I answered noncommittally.

He looked from me to the closed elevator doors. It only lasted for a moment, but I could sense he had a question in his head. Something didn't seem right to him.

I drew his attention to a sign showing the location of our room. "I think we're down here."

I repositioned the ice bucket against my chest. "Do you have the key card?"

"Yep."

"Then let's go. We've got a couple of hours until we're meeting everyone."

"Oh, really?" James asked with a naughty smile on his face.

"Gee, can you think of anything we can do to pass the time?"

"I can think of a few things," he said in a husky whisper, his eyes sweeping my figure.

I could feel his eyes on me as we strolled down the hall. Absence really did make the heart grow fonder. I grabbed the key card from his hand and slid it through the reader on the doorknob.

I held the door open for him as he yanked my heavy suitcase into the suite. Kicking the bag out of his way, he shut the door. He came up close to me, a light of desire flickering in his eye. He gently removed the shoe-filled ice bucket from my arms and set it on the floor. Pulling my body toward his with an aching gentleness, he pressed his lips softly to mine.

"I missed you," he whispered against my mouth. Then, he trailed kisses down my neck and slipped the strap of my sundress off my shoulder.

A slow ache built in my chest. I touched his face with my hands and guided his mouth back to mine, needing to feel his sweet kisses again. Everything about his lovemaking was gentle and quiet. He touched me as if I were a bird about to flutter

122

away.

He reached behind to unzip my dress inch by agonizing inch. His smooth, warm touch slid from my back to my shoulders, down to my waist—as my dress dropped to the floor.

Goosebumps rose on my arms in the air-conditioned room.

"Let's move you to the bed." He scooped me up in his arms and left my dress behind. The sensitive parts of my almost-nude body brushed against his clothes, and I wished he would rid himself of everything. I pressed myself to him, letting him know by touch alone how much I had missed him.

He carried me through the living room area, into the bedroom, and laid me gently on the bed. Then, he braced his hands on either side of me, looking down at me with pupils as large as a cat's. He swept his gaze down the length of my body, over my rounded breasts and down to the jut of my hip. He slid his finger into my panties and drew them down, agonizingly slow. My stomach quivered at the smooth slide of silk down my thighs and the heated warmth of his hands against my skin.

I felt adored, treasured, loved.

Kneeling above me on the mattress, he kept his darkened eyes on my now-naked body as he pulled off his shirt and unbuckled his belt. Then, half-dressed, he bent down to bring my nipple into his mouth. A warm swirl of desire rushed through me as he caressed me with his tongue.

I couldn't stay still any longer. I reached for the waist of his pants, pulling them down and off. I needed him inside me, I needed him to be part of me.

As he parted my legs with a slow sensuality, the memory of Joaquin's hand sliding down my hip, only to stop because of a phone call filled my head. He didn't stop because of my objections, but because of a phone call. James's phone call.

My breath caught in my throat. My limbs tightened. James brought his face up from my breasts.

He knew. He knew something was different, something

was wrong.

I curled away from him into a ball on the bed. Tears formed in my eyes. The guilt of what I had done was too much to bear. James touched me so sweetly, so kindly. His gentleness pained me. I knew his trust could be easily lost.

"Suzie?" he asked, pressing his body to my back. Keeping me warm, when I didn't deserve the warmth he offered. "What's wrong? Is everything ok?"

With one quick motion, I wiped a hand across my eyes and then reached for his hand. He let me take it and draw it over my waist. I said nothing. I wanted him close to me.

He curled up against me. I knew he wanted me to answer him. I imagined the thoughts running through his head. Thoughts of worry and doubt.

I pulled his hand to my breasts and left it there. He caressed their curved softness, and then he pulled me against him, so I could feel his erection.

I rolled over on my back and looked into his eyes. Those calm, green eyes that hid nothing.

"Kiss me." I strained my head toward his. I wanted him to kiss me hard. I wanted nothing gentle or sweet. I didn't deserve such gentleness.

His lips slipped softly over mine, and I pressed hard against his mouth, to show him what I needed from him. But he circled my wrists and pushed my arms against the bed, forcing me to slow down.

He dragged his mouth away from mine. We were both panting. I arched my body up against his, demanding he continue.

He let go of my wrists and stared at me, drinking in my naked body. But I saw confusion there, too. I never acted this wild with him. Never this rushed and harsh. We were slow and gentle together like water lapping at the edge of the shore, rushing in and out but always returning, always connecting, never letting go.

With my hands free, I reached for him. I pulled him back

down to me again, and we lost each other in a bruising kiss.

Darkness slipped in softly while we made love. Its shadows arcing across the bed, where we lay entangled and spent. James combed his fingers through my hair and sighed against my cheek.

He was content. He was in love.

I was frightened.

My heart fluttered against my chest, and I wished that I could still it with a single thought. A single, beautiful thought. *James loved me. James loved me.* The phrase echoed in my head.

Then I thought ahead to the party. The meeting with Joaquin. I worried my body would betray me. That James, as he touched my hair, my face, would feel the betrayal in me. One more lie I had to tell, and then it would all be over. After tonight, there would be no more lies.

James laid his hand over my chest, and we both closed our eyes in exhausted sleep.

Chapter Fourteen

"Suze, wake up."

I stirred in the bed, the sheet tangled around my naked thighs. My mouth had turned chalky and dry. "Hmmm," I mumbled.

I dreamed James and I were at home in our little green-and-white house on a Saturday morning. He was going to run out for coffee and muffins like he always did.

"It's time to get up for the party." He shook me by the shoulder. "Janice will be waiting for us. Remember? We're meeting her at the pool?"

I bolted awake. "What time is it?" I rubbed my heavy lids.

"Six-thirty. We didn't sleep very long."

I looked over at him, the bedside lamp bright in my unadjusted eyes. He sat at the foot of the bed. "And you're already dressed? You didn't sleep at all," I accused.

He had donned khaki pants and a loose white linen shirt. Somehow the man who wore chinos, a button-up shirt, and loafers to mow the lawn, knew exactly what to wear to a party in Mexico? He made absolutely no sense. Every day held a new surprise.

I shook my head at the craziness of it all. The airport, the meeting in the elevator, the rough tumble in bed all mixed together in my head.

I got up, wrapping myself in the white sheet that had been in an untidy heap at my feet, and headed to the bathroom. "I enter a mess, but will come out a goddess," I announced.

"You're already a goddess," James said appreciatively from his spot on the bed.

That's when I noticed my whole back end was exposed to his view. I tugged the sheet around me and laughed. Even in this messed up, upside-down situation, James could make me laugh.

He peered at his watch. "Countdown t-minus twenty-five minutes and counting."

"Yes, sir," I giggled, giving him a salute. The sheet slipped down over my naked shoulder.

I ducked into the bathroom. Seeing my smiling face in the mirror, my hair mussed from lovemaking, I felt a fraud. I was a liar.

I turned away from the mirror and leaned heavily against the sink, thinking about the night ahead of me. I had to look my best tonight. I didn't want Joaquin accusing me of not playing the role of devoted wife to the hilt. He would get one shot to do whatever it was he wanted to do, and then he would give me what I asked for. He promised me that he would.

Only a few more hours and the lies would end.

*

"Did someone say there's going to be a party?" announced James when we showed up on the patio.

The moonlight glittered prettily on the smooth water of the Olympic-sized pool. Tiki torches dotted the patio, their hot orange flames lighting the way to the open bar. Several tables sat to one side covered with trays of appetizers and enormous fruit sculptures crafted from melons, pineapples, and mangoes. Small clusters of hotel guests chatted, and a mariachi band warmed up on a stage near the bar.

Janice, her lithe body wrapped in a bright blue swath of filmy fabric, held up her margarita glass. "It's already started." Wearing black stiletto heels, she towered over her date. But neither seemed to mind.

George stretched out his hand to James. "Hey, good to see you guys again." He gave James a punishing handshake as evidenced by the wince of pain on James's face.

A professional white water rafter did not give wimpy handshakes, apparently.

After exchanging pleasantries, James excused himself from the group to grab us a couple of umbrella-decorated drinks from the bar.

Janice grabbed my arm, her voice high and shrill with excitement, "Did you get a chance to introduce James to Joaquin yet?"

My face blanched at the thought. I couldn't even imagine what James would say if I introduced him to the supposed 'stranger' we met in the elevator and nonchalantly mentioned that he used to be my boyfriend. God, and not to mention that he was my damned husband. I found myself in a demented episode of *I Love Lucy*, but without the laugh track. What I wouldn't give for it all to be over after a couple of rousing songs at the Tropicana Club with Desi and the band.

Instead, I offered up an excuse, "I haven't seen Joaquin so far. Have you?" I hoped beyond hope Janice hadn't seen him either. I bet on the fact she only had eyes for George tonight.

"No," Janice said, distractedly.

George had wrapped his arm around her waist. Janice was on the verge an out-an-out old-fashioned faint. In the last few days she had fallen hard for her Greek rafting god. Behind the fluffy blue dress beat the heart of a practical lawyer, but it was hard to tell when she made cow eyes at her new beau.

Lucky for me, she was so focused on her date. It would keep me out of her head. Me and Joaquin.

Later, when I needed to slip away, Janice would be one less

person I would have to worry about. Especially now that she had the suite all to herself. In fact, judging by her current behavior, I wouldn't be surprised if she left the party early for a private party of her own with George.

"Here you go, Suze," James returned with two coconuts filled with some kind of alcoholic drink. He handed me the one with a bright pink umbrella.

I had a plan—a lousy, horrible plan, but it started with that one drink.

James wasn't a big fan of alcohol, but tonight he would be. The only way to make sure he wasn't around, wasn't awake, wasn't conscious when I met up with Joaquin later than evening was to make sure he got smashing drunk.

The mariachi band tuned their instruments, and I settled in for a long evening of pretending to drink, pretending to enjoy the band, pretending to be happy James was here with me.

"Come on, baby, let's show off our moves" George pulled Janice into the small crowd of dancers by the pool.

Janice handed me her margarita. "Just watch what these feet can do!" She disappeared in a swirl of blue fabric.

"You want to give it try?" James asked me as we watched Janice and George kick up their heels.

I took a huge gulp of my coconut drink. "With a little bit of liquid courage, anything's possible." I let him lead me out into the crowd of dancers.

*

"Are you sure you guys are going to be all right?" Janice asked me.

Several hours and way too many drinks later, James tottered on his feet. His usually neat, light brown hair was mussed and drooping over one eye. He carried his loafers, having removed them to wade in the shallow end of the pool, and the cuffs of his pants flapped wetly against his ankles.

James leaned heavily on my shoulder, "We're juss perfek, Janny-wanny." He gave a sloppy smile and then kissed me hard on the cheek. "Juss perfek, right babe?"

James never called me 'babe.'

I tried my best to keep up the illusion I had gotten as drunk as my date. Most of my drinks I had surreptitiously tossed in potted palms or dumped into James's glass when he wasn't looking.

I grabbed onto a chair for support and mumbled, "I'm tired." I half-closed my eyes and stumbled a bit.

Janice bought it, but she was probably almost as drunk as we were. George had helped my plan along considerably by suggesting we do a toast after every song the mariachi band played. By nine-thirty George had begged off the challenge, and James splashed around in the pool.

The next step in my plan involved helping James up to the suite, pretending to fall asleep, and slipping out the door for my appointment with Joaquin. It would work. I had gotten this far without any trouble. James was falling down drunk. Janice was hanging all over George. It couldn't be more perfect.

I tripped over my own feet and held on to James. We were Siamese twins attached at the rib cage. Lumbering into the elevator, I pressed the button for our floor. James chuckled.

I looked sideways at him through my hair—once elaborately pinned up, but now hanging limply around my face. He had caught sight of our reflection in the shiny gold plating that lined the upper-half of the elevator.

"Oh, my God," he said, laughing, "I am so wasted, and I'm in Mexico."

"Trust me," I said, dumping the fake-drunk thing, "you aren't the only drunk person in Mexico."

We reached our floor, and the door slid open. Dragging my fiancé down the hall to our room turned out to be harder than I imagined. The fact he was being uncooperative didn't help matters any.

"Could you try picking up your feet a little bit?" I asked,

exasperated. His bare feet moved like lead weights across the softly carpeted hall. Right at the door to our suite, key card in hand, he stopped dead in his tracks.

"My shoe?" He looked quizzically at the lone loafer in his hand. Somehow, he had managed to drop a shoe without either one of us noticing. He swung his head in a jerk to look over his shoulder. "Hol' on. I'll get it." He made a move to lurch out of my grasp—the grasp that kept him from falling to the floor in a drunken heap.

"Whoa, kemosabe," I said. "Let's get you inside. I'll get your shoe, okay?" I slid the key card through the reader with one hand and clamped down on James's shoulder with the other.

He was in no condition to protest. He nodded his head and gripped the door frame as I tried to move him into our room. "My shoe—"

"I'll get it," I said, my voice becoming sharp. I shoved at his solid body, determined to get him in the door and in bed. His fingers slipped, and his body sagged. I leaned on him hard like a football tackle would a dummy during practice. My weight propelled him forward into our darkened room. One final grunt, and he lay sprawled across the couch, eyes closed, snoring, and holding onto his loafer.

"I'll get it," I whispered. I headed out into the hall to retrieve his lost shoe. The door closed behind me, and I was alone in the quiet hall. My ears rang from the loud beat of the mariachi band, and my throat was dry from all the drinks I didn't drink that evening.

I walked down the hall, picked up James's shoe, and held it in my hands for a moment. Then, I leaned against the wall and cried.

*

An hour later I left our suite. I had upswept my hair neatly and had freshly applied my make-up. My eyes were no longer red. Thank goodness for Visine.

I left James in the room exactly as he had landed, looking like a beached whale on top of the couch in the living room. I had been afraid to try moving him to the bedroom or taking off any of his clothes. He only needed to sleep for an hour more, and then I would be back.

It would all be over soon.

I yearned for that weight to be lifted from me. Twelve years of wondering and worrying and waiting. I should have gotten the divorce years before I'd ever met James. But how did I know I would find such a wonderful guy? How did I know that love wasn't over for me the minute I stepped back in the United States? I had been ridiculously young and had no idea what waited for me down the road. And now I was paying for that mistake and all the lies.

I waited at the elevator for the door to open, half-expecting Joaquin to be waiting inside. My heart ratcheted up a few beats. I headed into the unknown. I had to play the wife, but why and for whom? Did I really care?

I caught sight of myself in the gold plating, like James had earlier. My face looked thin, distorted. My mouth was a straight line of worry.

The elevator stopped a few floors down, letting on two older couples. I relished the interruption and was glad their bodies blocked the revealing gold plating. I didn't want to look at myself so closely any more.

We reached the lobby in record time, and I plastered a smile on my face. I wanted to appear to be the happy and contented wife. Joaquin's wife. I had been a wife for twelve years, but had no idea how to act like one.

I headed to the meeting place, the couches in the lobby flanking an enormous indoor fountain. I saw him there. Waiting for me. His hand reaching out to me.

I took a breath and headed right for him.

Chapter Fifteen

That day at the pyramids, I managed to give Janice the slip. I went into the restrooms at the Teotihuacán Visitor's Center and never came out.

After about fifteen minutes, I heard her call out my name a few times. I even hid from her when she came looking under the stalls.

I should have been honest with her. It would have been better to tell her I was meeting Joaquin. But I was weak. I couldn't bear to see the hurt look on her face when I broke my promise. My insides churned at the deceit. Who does that to a good friend? Why couldn't I have been honest with her? She might have understood why I wanted to spend time with Joaquin and not with her.

Too late for that. If I told her the truth now, I would lose the only friend I had down here in Mexico.

After a few minutes of searching, Professor Burnham convinced her I was probably with the rest of the group or that I would catch up with them. Not as if anyone could miss a group of twenty American college kids wearing Vincent College t-shirts.

Ten minutes later, I came out of the bathroom and waited

for Joaquin to find me near the entrance to the Visitor's Center—our designated meeting spot.

It wasn't long before he showed up, looking handsome in jean shorts and a striped shirt. I felt a tingle of pleasure that this exceedingly handsome man was here just to see me.

"Let's take a walk." He grabbed my hand and tugged me through the crowds of tourists milling around.

"Where?" I had been under the impression we were going to hang out at the Visitors' Center for the few hours we would have to spend together.

"Let's hike up one of the pyramids." He squeezed my hand.

We spent the morning tackling both pyramids. First, the shorter Pyramid of the Sun and then the Pyramid of the Moon at the other end of the Avenue of the Dead. Both were steep with steps that went on forever. The hot sun beat down on us, draining my energy.

The Pyramid of the Moon had been a much harder climb than the last one, and the furthest from the Visitors' Center. I could understand why, once a tourist made it to the top of the first one, he had no energy to climb the next. Besides the heat, Mexico City and Teotihuacán were at an altitude of well over 5000 feet. My lungs burned at the lack of oxygen.

When we reached the top, Joaquin and I sat down to catch our breath. Perspiration dripped down my back.

A few brave souls were making the ascent, so we would only have a few minutes of privacy. We stood looking down at the Avenue of the Dead, the sun high and hot in the clear sky above. My throat was parched, but the soda vendors were a world away beneath us. My thirst would have to wait.

"Suzie," Joaquin pulled me down to the stone blocks to sit with him.

The wind picked up, and I shook my hair away from my face, letting the dry air cool my sweaty face. Slipping a stubborn strand of hair behind my ear, I looked at him, waiting.

"Do you love me, *querida?*"

"Of course," I answered without needing to think. Joaquin was handsome, intelligent, caring—how could I not love him? I wanted to spend every free minute I had with him. I looked around at the vista before us. There were brilliant colors, wind, sunlight. Sensation overwhelmed me.

"I have been thinking about you going back to America, back to your life there."

"I don't want to think about it."

"That's exactly it."

"What do you mean?"

"I don't want to think about it, because I don't want it to happen."

"I don't either, but I have to go back. The semester ends, I start my junior year next year. And you? You'll be finishing up your degree at UNAM."

"Yes." He paused. "But have you thought about staying here?"

"Maybe."

He reached out to touch my face gently. "Then why don't you?"

I pushed his hand away; I couldn't think with him touching me like that. "How could I do that, Joaquin? I'd have to renew my student visa, and you know how slow that process is. And there's no way my parents would keep paying my tuition if stayed down here. It wouldn't work."

"It could."

"How?"

"Marry me."

"What?" I held my breath. Us? Get married? I was only nineteen. My plan had been to finish college, get a job, find an apartment, lead this glamorous single existence in Chicago. Marry Joaquin? Stay in Mexico? That didn't quite fit into my plans. "I don't know—"

"I thought you said you loved me," he said petulantly. I'd never heard him speak this way. I wanted to please him, make him happy, keep his attention focused on me.

"I do. I do," I insisted. "But that's a lot to consider. That would change everything."

"I don't want you to leave me and go back to America, *querida*."

Several tourists finished climbing the steep steps and were now only a few feet away from our quiet spot. Seeing them, I realized the lateness of the hour, that my group would be expecting me. As much as I wanted to stay and discuss the idea, I had not time to think clearly about it, get some perspective.

"I need to get back to the bus." I looked at my watch. "It's twelve-thirty now, and we've got a long walk."

"Wait, you still haven't answered me. Will you marry me?"

His warm hands entwined with mine, his clear hazel eyes searched mine for an answer.

Me, get married? I didn't want to contemplate leaving Mexico and leaving Joaquin behind, but what exactly did I want from this relationship? How would this work out? I had wished many times over the past few months I could stay behind in Mexico, so didn't that mean I also believed Joaquin was the man I had been looking for? The one I would want to marry? And if that were true, what would be the point in waiting for three or four years, navigating the difficulties of a long-distance relationship? We loved each other, he wanted me to marry him, why not? What other answer could there be to his question?

The tour bus, my class, Professor Burnham, even Janice I pushed to the very back of my mind. They could wait a few more minutes, but my answer could not.

"Okay, let's get married."

"*Te quiero*, Suzie." He smiled and gave me a quick kiss on the lips.

"*Te quiero*."

It felt good being next to him there on the pyramid. He and I sat together, nothing in our way, all of Mexico laid out before us.

On the walk back to the parking lot, we hardly spoke, just enjoying the moment of being newly engaged. I had no ring, and neither of us had any idea of how or when any wedding would take place. We knew that we loved each other and from that moment on nothing would separate us.

*

When I got back to my dorm, I itched to tell Mercedes my news. That would shut her up once and for all.

But the minute I walked into my room, I knew something was wrong. What happened to the portable TV on the bureau? Where was the whirlwind of clothes Mercedes usually left behind before she went out on a Saturday night? Her bed had been stripped of its sheets, the books had vanished from her desk, and even her alarm clock was gone.

I set my backpack down on my neatly made bed. Where would she have gone?

Cristina, one of my suite-mates, popped her head in, commenting off-handedly, "*Mercedes se fue.*" Then, shrugging her shoulders at me, she disappeared back into the shared living room to turn on her favorite *telenovela*.

Mercedes left? Left for where?

Before I could ask Cristina what else she knew about my missing roommate, the loudspeaker squawked, "*Telefónica para Señorita Eisenhart. Telefónica para Señorita Eisenhart.*"

That was me!

It could be a call from Joaquin.

Putting on my shoes, I ran past Cristina who was immersed in the tortuous life of a beautiful washerwoman in love with a man twice her age and a hundred times richer. She didn't even turn her head when I opened the door and walked out to the stairs on the outside of the dorm building.

Our suite occupied the third floor, which gave us a fantastic view of the mountains, but when it came to answering phones, it was a pain in the neck. My feet scrambled down the steps, the ironwork railing rattling loudly with each footstep. Dashing through the courtyard, I dodged several students and scattered a flock of pigeons clustered on the lush, green lawn.

Slowing down near the guard shack, I tried to catch my breath as I eased open the glass doors. "*Soy Señorita Eisenhart. Teléfono para mí?*"

The guard, his stiff-brimmed hat too large for his head, nodded briskly and pointed at the phone labeled #2 on the counter.

"Hello?" I anticipated the rich tones of Joaquin's voice.

"Suzie? Is that you?"

"Mom?"

"We haven't heard from you in such a long time. We were worried. How are you doing?"

My father probably would have started this conversation differently. He would have opened with a bad joke and then asked if I had gotten Montezuma's Revenge yet. My mom? Well, she was definitely the practical half of the mom/dad team. She paid the bills, organized the house, kept track of everyone's calendar, knew every important phone number by heart.

"I've been busy. In fact, we got back from a field trip a little while ago, and I'm exhausted."

"Oh, did you have a good time?"

"Yes," I answered tersely. "Look, Mom, I'm tired. Could I call you tomorrow sometime?"

She paused on the other end of the line. "Sure, honey." My mother's voice sounded quieter than usual, maybe even a little defeated. "That would be fine. I understand you're busy. We're so used to having you nearby; we miss you so much."

"It's not as if I were home all the time when I was at Vincent."

"But you did come home every once in awhile."

"To do my laundry."

"You drove four hours just to do laundry? I hope that's not the only reason you came home."

"Of course not, Mom, you know I miss you guys. But there's so much going on here."

Being an only child, my parents had no younger sibling left behind to soften the blow of my going to college. My father often told me how empty the house felt when I had gone away to school. I imagined it had felt even emptier since I left for Mexico last August.

"I know, honey. It's just your father—well, it's hard for him, you know. His baby's gone, and he doesn't know what to do with himself anymore. Could you try to call back in a couple of hours? He'll be back from the gym."

"Why don't I call tomorrow night? When I'm not so tired. I promise." I made a mental note not to forget. Sundays were uneventful on campus, so I was certain it wouldn't be a problem.

"If you're sure."

"I'm sure." Okay, this was getting a little ridiculous now. What were they going to do when I graduated from college and moved out for good? I mean, I loved my parents and all, but this was good practice for them, me living here.

Then I realized, I *was* staying here. I would be marrying Joaquin, and I wouldn't be going back.

How could I explain to my parents how I met this guy, fell in love, and got engaged without them ever meeting him? My mother would think I dropped off the turnip wagon. My dad? Well, he would probably worry like crazy, but tell more of his silly jokes so I wouldn't know how he really felt.

"Sunday night, then." My mother answered, not sounding completely convinced I would remember. "You know we love you, honey."

"Yes, Mom. I know."

I hung up the phone and left the guard shack. When would I be able to tell my mom and dad? How would I bring up the topic? Maybe it would be best to say nothing. Then, I wouldn't have to face disapproval from Mom and worries from Dad. His only daughter getting married at nineteen? Not quite what he envisioned.

Lost in thought, I felt a touch on my shoulder and almost jumped out of my skin.

"Hey, Suze! I called your name, like, ten times. Where are you? On Mars?"

It was Janice, a mask of red splotching her cheeks and nose—she had forgotten to put on sunscreen before our excursion to the pyramids. She never tanned; only stayed sickly white in the winter or burned as red as a lobster in summer. The harsh sun of Mexico had done quite a job on her.

"What?" My mind snapped back to the people and noises around me, my parents momentarily forgotten. "Oh, sorry. I have a lot on my mind."

"Where the heck did you disappear to today? I didn't even see you get on the bus."

"I couldn't find you either." Oh, what a good liar I'd become. "I went in the bathroom and when I came out everyone had gone. I ended up walking the place by myself."

"Oh, no! Was there more than one bathroom? I called and called for you—and I never saw you anywhere."

"I don't know. I was lucky I made it on the bus at the last minute. I had to sit up front with the professor."

Janice's thin mouth curved into a frown. "Why don't we go to the cafeteria and get some fried bananas? I'm bummed we didn't get to spend the day together."

"All right, but I'm buying." It was the least I could do for her after lying to her.

"There's no way I'm gonna turn *that* down." We left the dormitories and headed toward the cafeteria across the center plaza.

"And tomorrow, let's go to the movies—just you and me," I added. I needed to start acting like a friend again.

"Okay!" Janice gave me a hug.

We entered the cafeteria, the lights blindingly bright after our walk in the semi-dusk. Getting in line, Janice had to ask me one last question. Just as I was feeling more like myself than I had in weeks and starting to relax and forget all the people who depended on me to be good old, well-behaved Suzie.

"I ran into Cristina when I was looking for you earlier. She said Mercedes moved out, dropped out of school. What the heck is going on?"

Dropped out of school?

What had happened since I left her this morning? We certainly weren't the best of friends, but Mercedes and I could be civil to one another.

"What?"

"Yeah, guess she was real upset or something. She didn't want any help packing up, didn't talk to anyone. Weird."

Weird was right. But at least she wouldn't be interfering anymore with Joaquin and me. I was relieved to have her gone. No matter what the circumstances were.

Good riddance, Mercedes, wherever you are.

Chapter Sixteen

I stood by the indoor fountain, waiting for Joaquin to arrive. My red heels were pinching my feet. Too many salsa dances, I supposed.

"*Querida.*" Joaquin came up behind me. He snaked his arm around my waist, taking possession of me.

"Don't call me that," I said. "Never again." The warmth of his hand burned right through the thin material of my dress, but I let him keep it there. I had to play my part. I wouldn't let him renege on our deal. I would do what he asked.

"All right," he said coolly.

Through the huge glass doors at the back of the lobby, I could see quite a crowd around the pool. My ears pricked up at the familiar rhythm of the mariachi band. I wished I could be outside again next to James, Janice, and George with the moonlight in my hair and the tropical breezes at my back.

"Here we are." Joaquin led me through the tall double doors of a ballroom right off the lobby. In the ballroom a more exclusive party had gathered. Tables covered in pristine white tablecloths dotted the room. Wait staff in formal wear carried trays of caviar and shrimp.

"What's going on? This isn't the party." He had misled me.

I thought we would be sipping cocktails and making small talk out on the patio in a more casual setting.

Joaquin signaled to a slim man in a very expensive suit who stood near a small crowd of people. "Enrique!" He had a huge grin on his face.

Enrique, a slight man sporting a thin moustache, returned the smile and nodded at Joaquin. Then, his gaze riveted onto me. The neat moustache over his upper lip curled up on one side, as if his interest had been piqued by my appearance.

Enrique left a group of people and headed straight for the two of us.

A nervous flutter tickled my stomach. More was going on here than a simple party. My play-acting had a larger purpose than Joaquin had led me to believe.

"*Cómo estás, Joaquin?*" Enrique enthusiastically greeted, clapping Joaquin hard on the back. "*Y quién es la bonita señorita?*"

Joaquin spoke in English, "This is my wife, Suzette." His hand around my waist burned.

"*Tu esposa?*" Enrique choked out the word.

Joaquin ignored his look of surprise. "This is Enrique Guzmán, our marketing director." He nodded at me, encouraging me to interact.

I stretched out my hand, "How good to meet you, *Señor* Guzmán."

Enrique grasped my hand limply. He didn't seem to know what to do with me. He continued to stare at me as if he had never seen an American woman before.

Our little group must have attracted some attention because more people approached us, listening in to Enrique's questions.

"Have you been in Acapulco long?" Although his accent was thick, Enrique's English was quite good.

I hesitated, looking up at Joaquin, not sure how to answer.

"We've been married almost twelve years, Enrique," Joaquin laughed off the question.

Enrique reddened.

I wanted so badly to look at my watch to see how much more of this I had to sit through. A tray of hors d'oeuvres came by, and I reached out for something to eat. Anything to get my mind off of the man staring at me. Even in his embarrassment, Enrique never took his eyes off of me.

Once Joaquin made his announcement, the small crowd of people gathered around us went silent. A nervous tinkling of glasses rang out.

"*Dónde estabas*, Joaquin?" a rich, feminine voice called out from behind us.

A slow, wicked smile appeared on Joaquin's face, and he turned us to face the woman who approached.

A familiar cloud of thick, black hair surrounded a face I would have recognized anywhere. She was a little bit heavier, but as beautiful as the day she disappeared from the university.

"Mercedes?" I am sure my face went as pale as a ghost. I turned to look at Joaquin.

A fit of nervous energy ran through my body. Joaquin's hand at my waist clamped more tightly. His malicious smile grew wider.

"I was meeting my wife," Joaquin said, his voice placid and smooth, as if he were talking about taking a trip to the grocery store.

"Your wife?" Mercedes gasped. "What is she doing here?" She looked pointedly at me, her eyes narrowing.

"We are moving to America. I'm leaving you. I'm leaving Acapulco." He let go of my waist and gripped my hand instead.

"Then it *is* true," she said. "You really did marry her? It wasn't a lie?" Mercedes looked to me for confirmation.

I nodded.

This was what he needed me for. As an escape. As a way out. But when did he and Mercedes get together? After I left for home?

All those years I worried about Joaquin's state of mind,

and he had moved right into another relationship without a thought about me.

"I told you the truth, Mercedes. I'm not a free man. Now you can see for yourself."

When I had seen Joaquin in the hotel lobby days ago, I thought his expression had been one of hurt and anger. But now I understood he had been hatching his plan even then. I stepped back into his life out of nowhere, and he found a way to take advantage. To hold the divorce over my head, when he probably didn't care one way or the other if I stayed married to him.

The crowd tensed around us, listening closely to the domestic situation unraveling right before their eyes.

"You're leaving Acapulco? Leaving Mexico?" Mercedes's deep brown eyes lost their spark. "But what about Ariana? You will leave her, too?"

I remembered the girl in the photo in Joaquin's office with her eyes so like his. Mercedes was Ariana's mother?

Joaquin let go of my hand. He stepped forward and grabbed Mercedes by the upper arms. His fingers dug deep into her flesh. He whispered, but not so soft that I couldn't hear, "This is over, Mercedes." He thrust her away from him, and she tripped backwards into a table. Stumbling for a moment, she caught herself.

Her eyes penetrated mine. Pure venom flashed in their coffee-hued depths. "His wife," she spat out. Her gorgeous hair radiated from her cruel face in soft waves. "Did you know that he was with me the whole time? When you were making all those stupid plans? He didn't love you. He never loved you."

Mercedes words hit me like a sack of bricks. The years I had wasted wondering if I'd made a mistake. Wondering if Joaquin missed me, worried about me. It had never been real. None of it. The shame of it burned me. What a little fool I'd been. What a stupid little nineteen-year-old fool.

"Ah, but I married her, didn't I, Mercedes? I married *her*."

Joaquin grabbed a glass of champagne off of a waiter's tray as it passed by.

The crowd parted behind us. Someone made her way through the small gathering of people surrounding us.

"Is it true, Suzie?"

Janice's face paled and her thin lips trembled. "Are you married to Joaquin? Are you his wife?"

Where did she come from? I thought Janice had gone back to her room with George. How did she find us?

Oh, God. James.

My blood ran cold as ice in my veins.

She can't tell James.

"All those years ago—when you stood me up—you were married to him and didn't tell me?"

I reached out for her, grasping at her arm, her hand, anything I could touch. But she pulled away from me. "No, it wasn't like that, Janice. I swear to you."

With a sheen of tears in her eyes, she shook her head and backed away. "You lied to me. You lied to James. You even lied to your own mother. How could you do that, Suzie? What kind of person are you?"

She melted into the crowd. "Wait! Let me explain." I yelled over the din in the ballroom. "I can explain. Please don't. Janice, come back!"

To finish my explanation would be useless. She'd headed straight out the door and probably right up to the suite James and I were sharing.

She loved James. She might have been my friend first, but she wouldn't keep something like this from him. Not after I had betrayed her, too.

My arms, still reaching out, froze. Panic trapped me there in that crowded, stuffy ballroom. Strangers pressed all around me, watching me as if I were a circus sideshow. I had entered the room on Joaquin's arm, and now I would leave alone and humiliated. I had no one here who cared about me.

Mercedes, her face a mask of anguish and rage, slapped Joaquin hard across the face. "You don't deserve to be a father, *pendejo.*"

Joaquin didn't react to the slap or the insult. His beautiful hazel eyes hardened. "*Vete,*" he barked, hands clenched at his sides. "It's over. I never wanted you. Never."

Mercedes turned away from him, graceful even in her humiliation. I had been frozen by my fears, and yet she managed to exit with her head held high, her face radiant and beautiful. To her, the last twelve years no longer existed. They were erased in an instant.

I envied her—the ease with which she walked away from the man who caused her so much pain.

I gave one last look at Joaquin. I saw now what I had never seen before—the cruelty hidden behind the sparkling eyes and sensuous mouth.

I thought about James up in his room, sleeping, believing I slept next to him. I needed to talk to him, tell him why I had lied, tell him I was sorry. Before it was too late.

James's single dimple flashed in my head, and I knew how much I needed to see him smiling at me again, his crooked, sweet smile. Meant just for me. How wrong I had been to make him wait for me all those years. How painful patience must have been for him. Yet he had endured it all for me.

For me.

My feet became lighter. I pushed through the crowd toward the open ballroom door. The heat of people pressing together bore down on me. I needed to be free. I needed to get away.

I exited into the lobby and didn't look back.

*

I ran into George on my way to the elevators. He flagged me down, concern etched deep on his face.

"Have you seen Janice? She headed for the restrooms ten minutes ago, and I haven't seen her since."

My thoughts were solely on getting into that elevator and

seeing James. I mumbled, "I have to go," and pressed the button on the wall to call the elevator.

George grabbed my shoulder, "Do you know where she is? Is she all right?" They had been drinking, it was late, and they were in a foreign country. I could understand his concern, but my mind focused on getting to James, on explaining myself to him.

The elevator doors slid open. I slipped inside, pressing the button for our floor. The doors closed, but George held them back with his hand.

"Is she all right?"

"She's fine. She's okay. She'll be back down in a minute, I'm sure," I snapped at him for no good reason. Anger at my own mistakes consumed me.

George stared hard at me and then shook his head. His hand slid off the door.

The elevator doors closed, and I slumped against the wall. I blinked my eyes to stop the tears from falling. I had no time to feel sorry for myself. I started this, and now I needed to own up to it. No more lies. No more secrets.

The doors opened on the fourteenth floor. I stepped into the pristine hallway. I welcomed the silence.

I wondered if Janice would be there when I got to our room. I knew it would be too late to tell him the truth myself. My feet refused to move any faster.

Up ahead, the door to our suite opened.

My heart skipped a beat. A flush of heat came over me. I had to keep moving forward. I couldn't stop now. I couldn't run away anymore.

A swath of bright blue appeared, and then the familiar, slim figure of Janice.

I was too late. The truth was out. The lies had caught up with me.

She closed the door and turned toward me.

I knew she saw me in the long, quiet hallway, but she looked past me.

As she came nearer, I could see her tear-stained face, her lips thin and tight. I stopped and watched her pass. The hem of her cerulean dress swirled around her straight legs, a mist of blue. I couldn't stay silent. I had to know.

"What did you tell him, Janice?" My voice sounded hoarse, ragged.

She said nothing as she passed me.

I raised my voice a notch, "What did you tell him?" My limbs shook.

Her footsteps faded away behind me. She gave no answer.

My feet carried me to the door. My mind became a fog of grief and longing. I wished I could go back years ago. The night when James changed my flat tire. When he smiled at me for the first time and revealed that dimple in his thin, dear face. I wanted to hold that day in my hand, like a precious stone, and keep it safe.

I smiled through the tears. I reached for that image in my mind and held onto it for strength. James loved me. He did. He truly did. And love was supposed to conquer all things.

I took my key card out of my purse and swiped it through the reader.

Chapter Seventeen

"So, have you told your mother yet?" I asked.

Joaquin and I lay out on the grass in Xochimilco one sunny February afternoon a few weeks after our engagement.

My head in his lap, he brushed tendrils of hair off of my face. "No."

"Why not? She's going to find out eventually."

"My mother wouldn't understand. She's worried that you will take me away from her. I already told you that."

"But she'll understand it even less if we keep it from her."

"Trust me. It's better this way."

Something about that statement made me uneasy for a split second. Had he only been interested in getting married to prove a point to his mother? But then I brushed that thought away. Of course not. His motives were the same as mine. I didn't want to tell my parents. I wanted to show them I was an adult. I could find, fall in love, and marry a good man all without them needing to approve of him. Besides, it had been so much easier not to let real life intrude on my romance. Talking to my parents would only take away some of the magic I'd found with Joaquin and the feeling of everything being right in the world.

"All right." I tilted my head back, angling for a kiss. He leaned down and obliged me, his lips tasting mine gently.

"And that means you can't tell your family either."

"I won't."

"I don't want them doing something to stop us. Keep us apart. I couldn't live without you."

"Oh, Joaquin. I know once I tell them, they'll love you."

"But right now, I want it to be just between you and me. No one else. Not yet, anyway."

"All right. I can do that." I planted another quick kiss on his mouth, and then sat up. My prone position on the grass was a little too tempting for us both.

"How about the first of May? That will give us time to get the paper work together, the money we'll need to pay the court."

"Money?"

"Eighteen hundred pesos."

Quickly working the math in my head, I said, "Four hundred and fifty dollars? Where are we going to come up with money like that?"

"We'll get it. Don't worry, *querida*. Nothing's going to stop us from getting married. I promise." He stared at me for a moment, and then a light turned on in those beautiful hazel eyes. "Hey, why don't we go to Acapulco?"

"Acapulco?"

"For *Semana Santa*, in April."

Semana Santa was the Mexican equivalent of Spring Break. Janice and I planned months ago to take a bus trip to the Yucatán and laze on the beaches of Cancún. It would be our last opportunity to see the country before the headache of finals and packing up for the trip home. Janice called it our "Last Hurrah." For me, it would be a way to make up for all the time I hadn't spent with her in the past few months.

"Just you and me—" he rubbed my arm slowly, "on the beach, in the sunshine. Nothing to worry about."

My breath quickened at his touch. Being alone, together

for one whole week without his mother, my friends, school?

"Let's do it." I was finding it way too easy to break my promise to Janice. Another one.

Smiling wickedly, he leaned into my body, giving me a slow, deep kiss that ignited a low-burning flame. If it weren't for the fact we were surrounded by people in a busy, public place, I might have slid my hands under his t-shirt to feel the warm hardness beneath. He had the most gorgeous body.

His hand crept up my arm again, softly brushing my skin, driving me mad with the possibility of us being alone. For a week. In a motel room.

I pushed him gently from me, and he groaned with a laugh, "You would do that."

"Do what?" I asked innocently, standing up and brushing grass off of my skirt.

"Make me want you more than I already do." He looked up at me from his spot on the grass, appraising my bare legs.

I smiled inwardly at his confession, glad to know I drove him to distraction. I would hate to be the only one suffering. I reached out my hand to help him up from the ground.

"I think I like the view from here just fine," he confessed, a lascivious grin on his face.

"Come on, I'm hungry." I tugged at his hand playfully.

"You're thinking of food at a time like this?" He got up off of the grass.

"No, but food might get my mind off of what I'm really thinking about."

We strolled toward a cluster of food vendors near the water, the brightly-painted kiosks striking against the washed-out blue of the late-winter sky. Young lovers strolled along the walkways, holding hands, whispering to each other. Just like Joaquin and me.

Were we the only ones planning to elope in this crowd of happy couples? Our secret settled heavily inside of me. I ignored the weight of it and led my fiancé toward a booth selling *pozole*.

"My favorite." Joaquin sat at the counter and took a deep whiff of the pork and hominy soup.

As we waited to be served, he looked over at me. "So, if we want to take this trip to Acapulco, that will cost us some money."

"Mmm, I suppose so." The cook behind the counter handed us our steaming bowls full of broth and succulent meat.

An idea formed in my mind, "I could cash in my plane ticket home. That would give us enough money to pay for the trip and the court fees."

To my mind, I wouldn't be going home anyway. In June, I would be Mrs. Joaquin Hernandez de León. I would be living with my husband here in Mexico City. I wouldn't need a ticket to the States. At least, not right away.

"Are you sure?" He'd half-emptied his bowl already, clearly worrying only increased his appetite.

"Of course, I'm sure. The ticket would go to waste."

A smile lit up his handsome face.

Our plans were coming to fruition. We only had to wait for the permission from the Mexican government for our wedding, and we had almost three months before we would need it.

"I'll get the money, and you make the plans." I blushed as I imagined what kind of plans he probably already had made for our trip.

*

"You're not going with me to Cancún?"

Janice and I were sitting together at a long wooden table in the library several days later, trying to do some studying before it closed.

"I can't, Janice."

"You can't? Or you won't?" Her eyes appeared watery, on the verge of tears. "I'll bet you're going somewhere with

153

Joaquin, aren't you?" She buried her nose in her Mexican history book.

"You know I don't want to hurt your feelings, don't you? But Joaquin and I—"

"Things have gotten serious, right?" The sarcasm in her voice was unmistakable.

"Right," I sighed, knowing I couldn't own up to the truth.

"And you don't have much more time to spend together, right?"

"Right."

"That's a load of crap, Suze." She slammed her book shut. The librarian sitting behind the front desk gave us a hard stare.

"What do you mean?" I whispered back, pretending to be deep into my Latin American Authors book to keep the librarian off our backs.

"I mean, we don't have a lot of time left to spend together in Mexico either."

"I know."

"You know, but you don't care." Janice pushed her book aside. She uncapped a pen and began doodling on her notebook, drawing pictures of palm trees on deserted islands.

"That's not true."

"Isn't it?" She stopped drawing and looked up at me, her expression flat, her eyes empty of their usual warmth and humor.

"I do care, it's just that—"

"Yeah, I know. I've heard it before enough times." She scribbled over the palm trees and islands, making a mess of her notebook page. "This weekend is Joaquin's birthday. This weekend is our two-month anniversary. This weekend Joaquin's taking me to a football game at UNAM," she mimicked in a sing-song voice.

"I know I'm spending a lot of time with him—"

"You're spending *all* your time with him." She was quick to correct me.

"I don't know what else to say, Janice."

"You don't need to say anything." She drew sailboats. "Anyway, Cristina invited me to come home with her for *Semana Santa.*"

"She did?" When did those two become friends? Janice's suite was in a completely different building.

"Yes." She added dolphins to her sea of sailboats. "I turned her down, but maybe, now that my situation has changed, the offer will still be available."

"Oh."

"Her family owns a house near Vera Cruz somewhere. Right on the water."

"Well, then, you won't miss me. Will you?" I closed my book.

"I guess not."

We sat there at the table for a moment, saying nothing. The anger hung between us like a living, breathing thing.

I stood up, unable to stand the weight of it. "I've gotta go." I scooped up my books and papers, shoved them in my backpack, and headed out of the library, leaving Janice to her maritime doodles.

Walking away from her, I felt horrible, but I didn't know how to fix what I already ruined. How could I ever make it up to her? I imagined after tonight, I would pretty much be on my own around campus. No roommate to hang out with, no American friends. I had been so neglectful of Janice she had every right to be angry with me, to be disappointed in me. If only I could explain to her how things were. What plans Joaquin and I were making. Then she would understand.

But I couldn't do that. She would certainly tell my parents.

The one thing that stuck out in my mind the day we left from Chicago last August was her promise to my parents—my mother especially—that we would watch out for each other.

*

"Girls, you need to be careful down there," my mother said to us in the airport, giving us the stern parent look.

My dad stood behind her with a bit of a smirk on his face. I wasn't sure if this meant he understood my mom was driving us crazy or that he agreed with her one hundred percent.

"Yeah, Mom. We get it." Geez, I hated it when she tried to be everyone's mom—not just mine. Janice didn't deserve a lecture from my mother. She had her own over-protective parents for that. Just because we gave her a lift to O'Hare didn't mean my mother had the right to include her in the usual Eisenhart lectures about safety and responsibility.

"Mrs. Eisenhart," soothed Janice, "you don't need to worry so much. The school takes every precaution. The university down there is guarded twenty-four hours a day."

I sensed my mother's defenses crumbling under Janice's brilliant logic. "You never can be too careful."

"We'll be okay, Mom. We're adults, remember?"

My mother focused her attentions on Janice, as if she were the only one paying any attention to her warnings. "You two need to promise me that you'll stick together. I don't want either of you going anywhere without the other, got it, girls?"

I sighed heavily and rolled my eyes. Parents could be so dense sometimes. As if I would go anywhere without my best friend.

"We got it, Mrs. Eisenhart." Janice gave my mother—my stoic, ramrod straight mother—a hug. And my mother hugged her back!

"Oh, girls, I'm going to miss you!"

Okay, where is the alien spaceship that abducted my real mother? My dad was the huggy one in the family. How is it that Janice could waltz in and get a genuine, loving hug from my mom?

"Let's go," I said. "The plane'll be leaving soon, and we need to check in with the group."

I pointed over at a large gathering of college kids wearing various Vincent College sweatshirts, t-shirts, and baseball caps.

Professor Burnham suggested we wear school apparel so that we were a "cohesive unit." Personally, I think we looked like a herd of cattle branded with a VC for easy identification.

"Ok, honey." My dad's eyes crinkled at the corners as he smiled at the two of us. "Guess we'll be seeing you next year. I hope you can remember how to speak English when you get back."

Then he gave me his biggest bear hug.

Chapter Eighteen

"Suzie, wake up. We're here," Joaquin gently touched my bare shoulder and whispered in my ear.

Groggily, I opened my eyes and lifted my head from his shoulder. Twelve hours on a bus to Acapulco was no way to travel—even if it was in the middle of the night. My mouth had run dry, my lids were swollen, and my left leg tingled from lack of blood flow.

"We're here?" I croaked, wishing bottled water was easier to find in Mexico. A tepid orange soda from a roadside stand at 2 a.m. didn't really quench a thirst. I stretched my arms above my head and tried to work the stiff kink out of my neck.

"*Sí, mira.*" Joaquin pointed out the tinted window next to me.

Though headed for the bus station and not the beach, the main road into town took us right past a most fantastic view of the bay. The sun, barely over the mountains to the east, touched the waves of the ocean, turning them into silver-blue tongues of fire. The sand appeared to be one uninterrupted line of smooth yellow. I imagined spreading out my towel on that sandy expanse, soaking in the sun, and doing nothing.

I had managed to cash in my open-ended return plane

ticket a few days earlier. Trying not to think of my mother's disapproval or Janice's hurt feelings when they discovered my plan, I stuffed eight-hundred dollars worth of pesos into the change purse I wore around my neck.

Half we put aside for the wedding ceremony next month, and the other half covered this trip to Acapulco.

Two bus tickets from Mexico City to Acapulco cost less than thirty dollars, and cheap hotels were available all over the city. I left most of the planning up to Joaquin. I handed him the cash we would need to make our reservations, and counted down the days until *Semana Santa.*

Seven uninterrupted days. No classes, no Janice, no nothing. Just him, me, and the double bed in the hotel room.

"Let's go." Joaquin took our bags down from the overhead bin. He had an excitement in his voice and an impatience in his demeanor.

He grabbed my hand and pulled me down the aisle, trying to get us ahead of the other passengers who were gathering their luggage.

I was too exhausted to care. My feet stumbled down the steps, and then I was engulfed in tropical air so dense with moisture, it suffocated me. And it was only eight in the morning.

Standing in the bus station lot, exhaust fumes spilling from all sides, Joaquin breathed in slowly and said quietly, "*Qué rica.*"

*

Our second-floor motel room faced the inner courtyard where a half-full swimming pool reflected the blue sky. A scattering of dilapidated lounge chairs hugged the cement edge.

This once had been a nice motel.

A young mother and her two shabbily-dressed children shared one of the few unbroken chairs. All three of them were somnolent under the heavy heat, staring blankly into the pool. I wondered what they were waiting for. Why did they choose to sit out in the heat instead of inside where the machine-cooled air was more breathable? Leaning against the iron railing, I waited for Joaquin to return with a new key. The first key we picked up at the front desk wouldn't open the door to our room.

I watched below as Joaquin crossed the courtyard. He flashed a smile at me and held up a key. I prayed this one opened the door. I needed to cool off before my head exploded. The humidity and heat were so overwhelming I felt surrounded on all sides, enveloped in a cloak of hot, sticky air that wouldn't move. I rubbed the back of my hand across my sweaty forehead.

Joaquin climbed up the stairs. He was also drenched in sweat. I could sense a certain excitement in him when he stood close to me—a tremble in his hand as he reached out to unlock the door, the quick movement when he grabbed my backpack and carried it into the room, his hot touch when he grasped my elbow to lead me inside.

Cool air from the air-conditioning unit inside our room buffeted me, replenished me. I sank onto the double bed in relief and lay back on the faded bedspread.

"*Querida.*" Joaquin looked down at me with those hazel eyes as hot as the sun outside. Their golden-green depths drawing me in, making me forget the sweat and the heat.

He lay down on his side beside me, drawing his hand down the length of my face in a soft caress. Kissing me with a kiss as a light as a butterfly's wings, I sighed at the feel of his mouth on mine. I wanted nothing more than this moment with him, far from all my worries.

The light kiss intensified. The pressure of his mouth on mine grew. He spread his body out over mine, and I felt the hardness of his erection against my leg.

He wanted me.

I no longer cared about anything but his the heat of his

body against mine. A different heat than the cloying, sweaty heat outside.

He gave me light kisses down my face and across my throat. I closed my eyes and shivered under the touch of his lips on my skin. Everything was raw heat, raw power, raw emotion. My body strained against his, forgetting for a moment that we were in a cheap motel room with scratchy sheets and an anemic air-conditioner.

He pulled the clothes off of my body. Cool air hit hot, moist skin causing goosebumps down my back and my legs.

Joaquin's hand slid to my breast, his mouth pressing down on mine, letting me know what he wanted. The sex was fast and hard, and I didn't care.

*

Joaquin loved the beach—the waves, the heat, the sun.

I hated every minute we spent outside the respite of the air-conditioning of our dank little motel room—the uncomfortably warm water, the burning sand that stuck to sweaty body parts. I survived on Fresca purchased from beach-walking vendors and any shade I could steal from hotel *palapas.*

Joaquin wanted me to swim with him. I couldn't stand the suffocating warmth of the tropical water, which wasn't much cooler than the ninety-five-degree air with its high humidity. But I swam for him. He wanted me to lie on the beach with him. The sun scorched my skin with its intensity. But I stayed on that towel for as long as he desired.

I wanted him happy on our little trip. I wanted him to see that we were good together. That I would do anything for him.

I couldn't go back to Janice, having spurned her plans for *Semana Santa,* and tell her I had a horrible time. I couldn't call up my mother and tell her I had squandered my ticket home to spend it in some lousy motel for a week of really hot sex and heat rash.

If I removed us from Acapulco, if I put us back in Mexico City or even in Puebla, everything was fine. But this blistering heat made me want to tear my hair out. It made me want to pack my backpack, climb back on that bus, and head back to my dorm room.

This is not what I had imagined. This is not what I had imagined at all.

Chapter Nineteen

"James?" His name on my lips was like water on a parched tongue, soothing and cool. "It's me," I whispered, moving forward into the darkness.

A ray of moonlight seeped through a crack in the heavy curtains at the window, illuminating the TV screen on a stand in the corner.

"You lied to me," he said. His voice came from somewhere near the couch.

"I know." Shame burned inside me.

"For six years you lied to me." He sounded disgusted with me. "What kind of person does that? What kind of person lies to her fiancé? I trusted you. I believed in you." His voice cracked.

Those words hit me like burning embers, each one stinging more than the last.

"I can explain—"

"Get out."

My blood ran cold at those two words.

"What?"

"Get. Out."

"James—" I pleaded.

"Get the fuck out of my room."

I had never heard James speak that way. Not to me. Not to anyone. Hot tears stung my eyes. I wanted to cry. I wanted to show him that I hurt, too. Instead, I stumbled toward the door, my hand searching in the blackness for the knob.

The door opened, and a blinding stab of light from the hallway hit my eyes. I stepped into the hall, not knowing where to go. The door clicked shut behind me, and I made my way to the bank of elevators.

I needed to get away. To be alone. To think things through. His harsh words stung me. The tears fell out of my eyes in a hot rush. I couldn't stop them.

I pushed the button for the lobby and waited for the elevator to take me down.

*

I wiped the tears from my face, and looked at my watch. I had to pull myself together.

It was past one-thirty in the morning.

I exited out into the desolate lobby. A young man dressed in a suit and tie stood behind the concierge desk, and a sleepy-looking guard leaned up against the wall near the entrance. The guard, with his cap pulled low over his eyes, barely even gave me a glance.

I still wore my evening dress, but it had wrinkled, and I felt a mess. I took off my high heels to soothe my aching feet, but also to make it easier for me to move undetected. The loud tick-tacking of heels on the lobby's marble floor would undoubtedly draw attention to me when I most wanted to fade into nothing.

Shoes dangling from one hand, I made my way outside to the patio around the pool. A few couples remained from the fiesta, dancing slowly in the darkness. All but one of the tiki torches had burned out. Waiters cleared away empty platters, wine glasses, tumblers, and used napkins, which were scattered around on the small outdoor tables. The bar had closed. A *guitarrón* player remained on stage, strumming softly, while the rest of the mariachi band packed up their instruments.

A warm, moist breeze greeted me when I came out onto the patio. I stood for a moment, letting the gentle wind caress my body, the skirt of my dress fluttering around my legs. At that moment, the impact of what I'd lost, what I'd done came rushing at me. I lost the one man I needed most. The one man who always had loved me and cared for me.

I imagined lying in our bed at home, the comforter pulled up over my legs and a mug of coffee in my hand. James sat next to me in his button-up pajamas, the kind my father wore, with little pinstripes and a collar and buttons all up the front. I used to tease him about those pajamas. How old he looked. As if here were someone's grandpa. We would laugh, and he would kiss me, feeding me bits of muffin in the early morning light.

Oh, what had I done?

I had been so stupid to think this would all go away so easily. How naïve I'd been to believe I could fly down to Acapulco and walk away with a divorce just by snapping my fingers.

I walked past the last few couples who danced on the patio. Pushing through the hotel gate, I made my way onto the beach. The sand was cool to the touch. Even with the warm breeze blowing, I shivered at the feel of the sand on my bare feet.

I had no destination in mind, only a need to keep moving. A need to keep walking down the length of the sliver of sand that hugged the curve of Acapulco Bay. A need to find a quiet and solitary place where I could get free of my thoughts and stare up at the moon.

*

There, on the sand, sat a familiar figure. The dark tumble

of hair and a certain proud jut to the chin told me I'd found Mercedes. Even over the loud crash of waves against the sand, I could hear her weeping.

At first, I thought to pass her by. I had been part of her public humiliation after all. She probably wouldn't want to have anything to do with me. But her tears stopped me. I knew at least a little bit of what she must be feeling. If I couldn't help her, at least I could be sympathetic. We'd both been played for fools.

"Mercedes?"

She wiped her nose and eyes, keeping her head turned away from me. "Leave me alone. I want to be alone."

"I thought maybe I could help."

She snapped her head around and glared at me. "Help me? The wife of Joaquin Hernandez wants to help me? How sweet. How kind. Yes, help the pathetic little Mercedes. The little *idiota* who thought she fell in love."

"I don't think you're an idiot." I sat down beside her on the sand, tucking my long skirt underneath my bare legs. "And for what it's worth, I came down to Acapulco to get a divorce. He never loved me, either."

"I don't believe you."

"It's true. You know all those years ago? He used me to get away from you." I hugged my knees to my chest. "How perfect was that? An American student going back to the U.S. in a few months? If I hadn't left on my own, I'm sure he would have found some excuse to leave me. I'm guessing he was trying to get away from his responsibilities. The girl in the picture in his office? Ariana? Were you pregnant when you dropped out of school?"

She sighed and pulled her hair away from her face. "Yes. Four months along. I didn't know what else to do. If my friends found out, or my parents—he promised he'd take care of me. But it had all been lies."

"Oh, Mercedes, you must have been so scared. I wish things could have been different between you and me. I might have been able to help."

"Did he ever say anything about me? About our baby?"

"No! If I had known—" I picked up a handful of the cool sand and let it run through my fingers. "Well, that's all in the past now, and I'm sorry. I should've been there for you, and instead—"

"We both were young, no?" She looked at me through a strand of hair blowing in the sea breeze.

"Yes, we were."

"Do you want to see a picture of Ariana and me?" She brushed the sand off of her hands.

"I'd love to."

Mercedes opened her handbag, pulled out a red leather wallet, and flipped it open. "This was taken last year at Christmas." She handed me a picture.

Ariana wore a beautiful red velvet dress, her black hair radiated like a cloud around her heart-shaped face. Mercedes stood behind her, hands on her daughter's shoulders.

"She's very pretty."

"Thank you."

Now that I knew Ariana was Mercedes's daughter, the similarities were so obvious. "I think she looks a lot like you."

"Except for the eyes. She has her father's eyes."

"Yes." I brushed my thumb across the picture. "But she's *your* daughter."

Mercedes nodded and took the picture from me, carefully tucking it back in her wallet. "So, he's not leaving Mexico?"

"Not with me. I don't know. Maybe he has plans."

"His mother lives here, you know. She knew about the baby. She wanted him to do the right thing."

"And then I came into the picture. No wonder she didn't like me."

Mercedes smiled. "She doesn't like much of anyone. She's a tough woman to love, but she adores Ariana. She's been a wonderful grandmother to her."

"Maybe that's all she needs."

"Yes, maybe." She put her wallet back in her purse. "So, you're going to divorce Joaquin. Then, what?"

"I'm engaged to someone else."

"*Americano?*"

I nodded my head.

"That's good. I'm glad you have found someone."

"Thanks. He's a good man." I thought about the night he had changed my tire, down on the greasy floor of the parking garage in his nice suit. "He'd do anything for me."

"Well, that is the kind of man you should marry."

"Yes. Yes it is."

Mercedes glanced at her watch. "It's getting late. I really should go. This night didn't turn out quite the way I was expecting." She gave me a glimmer of a smile.

"It was good to talk to you, Mercedes. I hope you find what you're looking for."

"Ah, I'll be okay." She picked up a pebble and threw it into the waves. "How do they say it? 'There's more than one fish in the sea'?"

"Exactly."

We both got up off the sand. She waved at me and headed back toward the hotel.

I wasn't ready to go back yet. I needed some time alone to think, but I was glad that I had made amends with Mercedes. We may never have been destined to be friends, but at least now we understood each other.

Joaquin had hurt both of us. In that way, we were allies.

*

I sat on the sand for hours. This late at night no one was out on the beach—just me, my thoughts, and the silver moon, slowly moving across the sky.

I knew what I had to do. There was maybe a chance for me and James, but I needed to stop feeling sorry for myself. Moping would solve nothing.

I looked at my watch. Three-thirty in the morning. Before I tackled any of this, I needed to get some sleep somewhere. Sleeping on the beach probably would not be the safest bet, and, besides, I was cold. Even seventy-degree weather can start to feel chilly if you're wearing a spaghetti strap dress with a steady ocean breeze at your back.

I made my way back to the hotel, which seemed to be miles and miles from where I stood—its distinctive electric-orange lights like a group of fireflies at this distance. At some point, I lost one of my shoes. I was too tired to go back for it, so I left the orphan shoe behind in the sand, as if I were Cortez marking Spain's territory with a flag. The spot where I decided to fix my broken life.

Trudging through the sand, my legs grew weary. The lights were as far away as before. I wondered absently if there might actually be a treadmill under all this sand. Clearly, I was sleep-deprived.

But I walked on.

The hotel lights got closer, my body grew more tired. By the time I reached the pool patio, I was ready to collapse. I staked out an empty lounge chair, covered myself with a couple of the thin, hotel towels, and promptly fell asleep.

*

"*Señorita?*"

Someone shook me—rather roughly, I thought. I groaned and rolled to one side.

"*Señorita, no puede dormir aquí. No puede, usted!*"

My tired eyes cracked open. The early morning light burned them.

An anxious maid leaned over me, her plump little body quivering in confusion.

Oh, God. It was morning, and I had fallen asleep outside by the pool.

I sat up, clutching one of the towels to my chest.

Last night the lounge chair had been the perfect solution. I had been so, so tired, and there had been a very comfortable looking chair waiting for me to lie on it.

But this morning, I realized the error. Early morning buffet breakfast by the pool.

It was still early, thank goodness. But a few crack-of-dawn type people were queueing up across the patio from me, waiting for pancakes, *huevos rancheros*, and tropical fruit salad. While waiting, they found my predicament quite entertaining.

I finger-combed what must be my atrocious coiffure and got up from the lounge chair with as much grace as possible. I tried to wipe the wrinkles out of my skirt. And my shoes! Whoops. I'd forgotten. I only had one shoe.

I reached for my handbag, pulled out my room key card, and waved it in front of the maid's face. I didn't want her to think I was some drunk who had wandered in from the beach last night. I was a paying guest.

With as much dignity as I could muster, I sauntered past the pool and the growing line of earlier diners and entered the lobby.

I headed to the elevators without thinking. I didn't care that I looked a mess, that my teeth needed to be brushed, or that I had sand in places I didn't want to think about. My first thought was to find James. I wanted to let him know why I did what I did and that I would fix it. I would get the papers signed for the divorce before I left Mexico. I needed to tell him I had never loved anyone but him.

On the elevator ride up I thought about James in the room last night. How final and sad he'd sounded. I had to show him our relationship could be fixed. I had made a mistake. A terrible mistake.

The doors opened on the fourteenth floor, and the eerie, suffused quiet of the hallway surrounded me. My bare feet padded down the hall on the soft carpet. I'm sure I left traces of sand on the floor with each step.

A maid laid a fresh copy of the New York Times in front of each door.

I wished I could turn invisible. It bore great resemblance to the 'walk of shame' from a frat house early on a Saturday morning. Everyone who saw you thought they knew how you spent your evening, and it wasn't spent playing chess.

The maid glanced at me, taking in my bare feet, sand dusted calves, and wrinkled party dress. But she didn't say a word. Guess she'd probably seen odder things happen in her tenure at the Playa Del Mexico. She turned back to her duties, making her way in the opposite direction.

I walked past with as much dignity as I could muster. I'd feel a lot better about the way I looked if my hair hadn't been such a ratty mess. Several hours of walking in a steady sea breeze was about as bad for the hairdo as riding in the back of a convertible.

I reached our room.

A flutter of panic stilled me for a moment. What if he told me to leave again? What if he wouldn't listen to me and my explanations? I couldn't lose him. Not now.

I slid my room card through the reader next to the doorknob. The green light snapped on. I pushed on the handle, and the door opened.

The bright light of the morning shone through the window, and I stepped inside ready to fight for James. Ready to give him all of me. Every piece of my history. Every mistake I ever made. I was ready to lay everything bare.

The door shut quietly behind me.

Chapter Twenty

What would my mother think?

I rode the bus heading back to Puebla when this thought came to my mind. Although it was only a few hours after the wedding ceremony, what seemed so right to me at the time, now felt impulsive. But here I was on the way back to the university to gather my things and start my new life as a married woman.

My father would probably take it in stride. His only child, married in a whirlwind ceremony in Mexico? How romantic, he would say. My impulsiveness could be traced back to him. He had proposed to my mother only a few weeks after they began dating. He told me more than once that 'when you know, you know.' He had told me the minute he had seen my mother across the room at a crowded fraternity dance that she was the one, even though she had been his best friend's date at the time.

I had known with Joaquin. In my arms at the civil ceremony it had all felt perfect. Yes, I was young. Yes, I wanted to finish school, but why couldn't I finish my studies in Mexico? The horrible trip to Acapulco had been far from my mind.

My dad could convince my mom I'd done the right thing. She would probably have a fit, and then my dad would calm her down. I had been so dependable in the past, she would say. I had been on the right track—good college, good grades. She would panic. She would think I had ruined my life.

But my dad could bring her back. He had big dreams when he had been young. The wandering spirit. My mother had been his anchor in reality.

Now I had my own husband to think about. What a crazy feeling. I was no longer a girl. I was a married woman with a husband who loved me.

This would be my last trip to the Universidad de América Central. I would be transferring my credits to the UNAM, where Joaquin attended school, for the summer semester.

Then, I would call my parents and explain to them everything that happened. How I wouldn't be coming back for summer vacation as planned. How I wouldn't be going back to my job at the Dairy Queen. Maybe they could come visit us this summer, get to know their son-in-law.

*

When I walked into my dorm suite, Janice waited on the couch with a pinched look on her face. The minute she saw me, her face paled.

"Suze, where have you been?" Janice blurted out, leaping up from the couch her slim arms reaching out for me.

"With Joaquin," I said quizzically. "What's up with you?"

Janice's face became paler than pale, her thin lips taut against her teeth. She held something back. "You got a phone call this morning."

"And?" I asked, setting down my backpack. "Who was it?"

"Your mom." She said this in a whisper, and then her hand flew up to her mouth. "Oh, God, Suzie." The agony in her voice made my blood run cold.

"Tell me" I knew something was horribly wrong. "What

happened? What did she say?"

Waiting even those few seconds for an answer had been agony. I had never seen Janice so serious, so pale.

"Your dad," she began, and I heard a loud buzzing in my ears. I could anticipate what she was about to tell me. "He had a heart attack last night."

I didn't hear the rest. I didn't want to. Dad had heart troubles for the past few years. Nothing too serious, we thought. He had a simple surgery to get rid of a blockage and some medicines that he took regularly, but I never thought that—

I sagged against the doorframe, my purse dropped to the floor. Then everything went black.

*

That same night I waited in the airport in Mexico City for my plane home. All of my bags were packed. The only thing I'd left behind was a shredded copy of my marriage certificate and the inexpensive gold band that was my wedding ring. I had planned on sharing everything with Janice before I left school for good.

I had no time to explain any of this to anyone. Professor Burnham took care of all the arrangements. I could barely think straight, much less figure out a way to tell Joaquin what had happened.

He would have to wait until I got back to the States. Once the funeral was over—

Then, a wave of sorrow hit me in the gut, making rational thought impossible.

My father was dead. My wonderful, doting, sweet-natured father was gone forever. My mind could not grasp it completely, no matter how many times I repeated the truth out loud. I'd landed in a horrible nightmare.

I had only spoken for a few minutes with my mother on the phone before I left for the airport. The conversation had been mostly tears and stray, meaningless thoughts about which tie Dad should wear or which dishes we should use for the buffet afterwards at the house.

One thing she said broke through the clutter of thoughts in my mind and stuck with me: "At least I still have you, sweetheart. You will be here for me, won't you? Always?"

I had never heard weakness or doubt in my mother's voice until that day. To hear her plead with me now broke my heart. As if in losing my father, she had lost part of herself.

I answered automatically, "Of course. Always."

That's when I knew I couldn't tell her. I could never tell her. The marriage to Joaquin may have seemed like the right thing to do yesterday, but today, the world had turned into an entirely different place.

Yesterday, I had been a carefree college student in love with a handsome, young man. Today, I was a daughter whose mother needed her most desperately.

I didn't even know the person who had existed that sunny Saturday afternoon in Mexico City, smiling in front of the judge, letting Joaquin slip the ring on my finger. That Suzie no longer existed. Joaquin would have to understand that.

Waiting in the Mexico City airport, I tried to force myself to call him, tell him where I was going, why I wouldn't be at the bus station in the morning. My heart had grown numb, it didn't want to feel any more emotions. If I had to explain my father's death to him and hear his heart break over the phone, I didn't think I could stand it. I barely had my sorrow in check, and I still had to make it through a four-hour plane ride, a funeral, and a long line of relatives, friends, and neighbors waiting to give their sympathies.

A phone call to Joaquin right now was out of the question. It could wait until tomorrow. When I had a chance to settle in, adjust to this new life without my father in it.

*

When I did finally get home, my mother enfolded me in her arms and we wept. No words passed between us that first day. There had been no need for them, we both were thinking the same thoughts.

When I didn't make that phone call to Joaquin my first day home, I thought I would make the call the next day. Not a big deal. He would understand once I explained it to him.

But then another day went by.

And another.

Helping my mother to plan the funeral took everything out of me. In her grief, my mother couldn't make any decisions; she needed me to lift that burden from her. I called the funeral home, the church, the florist, the organist. I called the caterer, the family lawyer, the secretary at his work. It all had to be done, and I had been the only one capable of doing it.

My mother spent those first few days curled up in bed, her head buried under a comforter. People called with their condolences, and my mother waved a hand at me when I brought the phone to her, a fresh glut of sobbing making even the most simple of conversation impossible.

Joaquin had been the last thing on my mind.

*

After the funeral, Janice called. She was in Puebla; the semester would be finishing up in a few weeks. After asking about my mom and myself, she brought up a topic I had been avoiding.

"Joaquin's been calling for you. I didn't know what to tell him." She sounded tinny and far away, but I knew she worried about me.

"I know," the guilt filling my voice. "I just can't—my mother—"

Every time I explained my actions to her, my thoughts returned to my father. His body lying in a casket. His warm hands now cold and gray, his face once so animated now sunken and lifeless. And my mother, an emotional wreck. A strong, focused woman reduced to constant tears and hiding in her bedroom.

I couldn't stand it anymore.

"Do you want me to tell him what happened?"

"No!" I couldn't believe I said it. "Don't tell him anything. I'll take care of it."

My mother shuffled past the living room, her eyes circled and puffy. She had been wearing the same nightgown, bathrobe, and slippers since I had gotten home. Her hair was wild, and her hands clutched at the front of her robe, as if she were warding off a cold breeze.

"Janice," I said with a sob, unable to hold it in any longer, "I have to go now." I hung up the phone before I could hear her answer.

"Mom," I called gently, crossing the living room in a few strides to catch up to her, "do you want me to make you some soup?"

Her blank eyes looked at me, unfocused, "Your father needs his clean socks. He can't go to work without his clean socks."

Putting my arm around her shoulders, I guided her back toward the stairs. "I'll get them, Mom. Don't worry. And then I'll bring you some of that soup."

She nodded slowly, and for a moment her eyes cleared. Looking at me, she cried, "Oh, Suzie, what are we going to do?" She gave me a tight hug and held me for a long moment. The strength left her body as she clung to me. "I need to get some rest."

"Yes, mom, why don't you do that? You can have the soup later. When you're feeling better."

She nodded and let go of me. "What are we going to do?" she mumbled. Tightening the belt of her bathrobe, she ambled up the stairs to her bedroom.

Before I entered the kitchen, I sat down on the bottom

step and hugged my knees to my chest.

"Yes," I said out loud to myself, "What are we going to do?"

*

For a few months, Joaquin sent letters. I never opened them. Not one. I didn't have the courage. Instead, I stacked them in the bottom drawer of my bureau, tied with a string.

By the end of August, the letters had stopped. School was starting up again, and I thought ahead to the new year. With my father gone, I decided to transfer to a college closer to home. Even months after his death, my mother wasn't the same person she used to be.

There were days where I felt guilty for what I did to Joaquin. There were days I thought about trying to find a way to dissolve our marriage, but I had no money and no real idea of where to begin something like that. As the months and years slipped by, it had been easier to pretend it had never happened.

Until I met James.

He had changed everything.

Chapter Twenty-One

Our hotel suite stood empty. The bed was a mess of tangled sheets, and wet towels had been piled in the bathtub.

James's suitcase was gone.

My God. He'd left. He'd checked out and left me.

My stupid too-full suitcase and my ice bucket of shoes occupied one corner of the room. He'd left no note, no indication of where he'd gone, nothing.

Trembling, I sat down on the unmade bed. My head slipped into my hands, its weight too much for me to bear. I'd been too late. He had gone. I had no opportunity to tell him anything, to explain anything.

Silent tears slid down my cheeks, and I let them come. I didn't wipe them away. I didn't grab a tissue. I sat there and let their wet softness glide down my face. What had I done? Oh, what had I done?

All that stupid time I'd wasted wandering on the beach last night. I should have spent it here, with James, trying my hardest to keep him with me. To explain myself. But I gave up. I left and gave up.

What kind of woman does that? What kind of woman leaves the man she loves?

I should have stayed and fought for him. For us. What an idiot I had been. I let the best thing that ever happened to me slip through my fingers while I was out taking a damn walk on the fucking beach. Sleeping on the goddamn lounge chair. What the hell was I doing?

Angrily, I wiped the tears away.

I stripped out of my dress and took a hot shower. As hot as I could stand. The sand and salt washed away down the drain. I took the soap and scrubbed my face, got rid of my streaked mascara. I wanted to be clean. I wanted to start this day anew.

If I couldn't have James, I would at least fix the problem I should have fixed years ago. For myself. Not for anyone. Just for me.

Wrapped up in a towel, I sat down on the bed next to the phone. "Room 1210, please." It was early, but not so early that Janice wouldn't be up and about. Could be she'd decided to take a run right now, but maybe—

"Hello?"

Hello indeed. That was George on the phone. George, in Janice's room. In Janice's *bedroom*.

"Hey, it's Suzie. Um, is Janice around?"

I could sense George tensing on the other end of the line. Last night we hadn't ended on the best of terms. "Hold on."

"Janice? It's Suzie."

I heard her mumbling answer, "Tell her I'm not here."

George cleared his throat. "Um, well—"

He was such a nice guy, he didn't want to tell me that she didn't want to talk to me. I had trounced on her heart, used her like no real friend would. "I'm coming down. I have to talk to her."

I hung up the phone before he could protest. I had no time to waste. I needed Janice to hear my apology and to understand how stupid I'd been. What a huge mistake I had made by not bringing her into my confidence all those years ago.

I needed her friendship now more than ever.

I threw on some clothes, my wet hair plastered to my

shoulders, and rushed out of the room. Today was not about looking good or playing the tourist, today was about saving the relationships that mattered the most to me. I hoped Janice would give me a few minutes of her time. Let me in the door.

*

"Janice, it's me. Let me in."

I knocked again on the door to her room. I could hear whispering and movement inside, so I knew she was there.

"Please, I want to talk to you."

The door fell open. George stood there, fully dressed, a pained expression on his face. I could see Janice standing beyond him next to the couch where we had shared our screwdrivers that very first day of our trip, laughing and making plans. Now, her face looked pale and tired.

George looked over his shoulder at her.

She told him wearily, "Let her in. It's okay."

Without looking at me, he held the door open. Once I entered the room, he stepped into the hall.

"I'll see you downstairs for breakfast in a few minutes," Janice said to George.

I scrutinized her face, as the door closed behind me, looking for some sign she wanted to hear from me, wanted an explanation. But her thin features remained tight. She wore more Janice-y clothing this morning—an oversized t-shirt and a pair of baggy Bermuda shorts. Her legs appeared even thinner and more stick-like than usual.

But before I could open my mouth, Janice said, "So, when were you going to tell me?"

I knew what she meant, but it was hard getting the words out.

Janice rolled her eyes at me. "About a little thing called a marriage? To Joaquin?" Her arms crossed tightly and her left foot tapped the floor.

"I wanted to tell you, Janice, oh, God, did I want to back

then. But I couldn't. I promised him I wouldn't—"

"How could you not tell *me*, Suze?" Her voice cracked. "I thought I was your best friend."

"You *are* my best friend, Janice." I reached out to touch her arm reassuringly, but she pulled away.

She looked up to the ceiling and took a slow, deep breath. "Yeah, right," she huffed. "First, you get married behind my back, and then you use me for a free trip to Mexico."

"Use you?" I said, aghast.

"God, Suze, you're a piece of work." Her mouth curled in disgust. "Do you really think I'm that stupid? That naïve?"

"No." I knew I had lied to her, but I didn't think how much that might hurt her. All the little lies I had told to get here. Each one had been another stab to her heart.

My worst fears were coming true. The truth came out, and my closest friend was pulling away from me. If Janice was this upset, how would James ever forgive me? I was a liar. A liar who had hurt the people I loved. What kind of person does that?

"You never were my friend, were you?" Janice choked on those words. I could sense her feeling of betrayal.

"Of course I'm your friend! If it weren't for Joaquin being here—"

"See what I mean? It's all about you. *Your* problems, *your* life. Who cares about Janice." She turned away from me and faced the view of the ocean.

I had to convince her. I couldn't lose my friend now, not when I needed her advice and help the most. "Do you think I'm really that cruel? That I don't care about you?" I tried to turn her away from the view. I wanted her to see my face and know that this time I was being honest.

She turned, but she hid her face from me. "Everything you've done since you've gotten here was all about you and your problems. Just like when we were at the university." She was right. Why would she expect me to act any differently a decade later? I showed her where my loyalties laid back then—

that day at Teotihuacán, my trip to Acapulco with Joaquin. Why would it be any different now?

I had let her down in the past. Put my feelings before hers. I had been stupid then, but I had matured.

"That was years ago. Another me entirely. I was an idiot. I was selfish. And I never did apologize to you for that."

She lifted her eyes to mine. The usual happy smile on her face disappeared, replaced by a frown of sadness and worry.

"So who is the 'me' here in Acapulco with me now? My friend? Or Joaquin's wife? Oh, or, wait, James's fiancé?"

James. The sound of his name cut me with an invisible blade.

"You told him." We both knew the truth, but I needed to hear it said aloud.

"Yes, I did. He deserved to know the truth, Suzie. He's too good for someone like you." Her eyes were blazing.

She spoke the truth. I couldn't deny her that. "You're right," I said. "I don't deserve someone like him."

I felt the tears coming again, and I fought them back. Crying wouldn't help matters. I needed to stay focused, or I would never get James back or my friend.

My knees trembled, and I collapsed onto the couch. I couldn't take this anymore. I needed her to understand me, and I'd only made things worse. If I couldn't win back her friendship, then I knew I couldn't succeed with James.

I heard a whisper of movement. And then Janice and those long, thin legs were next to me, sitting in the wingback chair.

"I don't get you, Suzie. Why would you do something like that? Did you think I wouldn't understand? You were my friend, and I wouldn't have done anything to jeopardize our friendship." I sensed a softening in her demeanor. A small hope grew in my heart that she might be able to forgive me for my transgression.

"It seemed like the right thing to do at the time," I explained. "But when my dad died—"

A light grew in her eyes, a light of understanding. Maybe she was beginning to see how I had gotten myself into this mess in the first place. It hadn't about me at all. It had been about everyone I loved.

"Your dad? Is that when you and Joaquin—?"

"Yes." Tears pricked in the corner of my eyes. "Do you see now why I couldn't tell you?"

"But after things got better at home, why didn't you say something then?" Her expression hardened again. She still saw me as the liar, the selfish one. That look in her eyes hurt.

"By then, it had been months. The lie had grown bigger and bigger. There never seemed to be a good time," I said, not even convinced by my own words. Nothing could ever truly explain why I had made the decision I did. "And then there was James."

"Yes, James." Janice echoed, deep in thought.

"And now I feel like such an idiot. Joaquin never really loved me—he used me to get back at Mercedes."

"What?"

"That's why she was there last night at the party. They have a daughter." I let that fact sink in for both of us.

All those years of worrying about what Joaquin had been thinking and feeling had been wasted emotions. He'd never thought of me beyond what I could do for him.

"I think that's why Mercedes left school back then," I told her. "I think she was pregnant. God, what an idiot I was for not believing her. She tried to tell me. She tried to. And I wouldn't listen. I thought she was jealous."

Janice sat back, her face reflecting disbelief. Then, came the Janice-type comment I had been hoping for, "What a bastard. What a friggin' bastard."

Janice didn't swear much.

"Yeah, pretty much."

She patted me on the knee, all of her best friend responses starting to come to the fore. "Dick."

She blushed when she said it.

I looked her straight in the eye. "Janice, I know I've hurt you. I know you feel I took advantage of you. I wanted you to know that's why I turned down the trip in the first place—I couldn't face you here, not after everything that happened between us in Mexico. I thought you would probably read it on my face the minute I stepped off the plane at the airport. But James insisted I go after you talked to him."

"He did?"

"He wanted me to take this trip because he doesn't think I know what I want. If I want to be with him, get married—"

Her brows knit together, "Oh, but you love him!"

"But he doesn't think I do," I divulged. I thought back to the conversation I had with James in the kitchen at our house. He thought this trip would be a way for me to analyze my feelings for him, get some perspective on things. "Especially not now. God, I don't know what to do. How can I get him back?"

"You need to find him, Suze."

I looked in Janice's eyes and saw reflected there her faith in me and in my relationship with James.

"He's already gone," I told her. "It's too late."

"It's not too late, Suze. He loves you—it's not too late." She reached out and grasped my hands in hers. I could feel some of the anger and hurt drain away from her in those cool, thin fingers.

"I have to take care of something first, though," I said.

Without having to explain further, I knew she understood what I meant. "He still loves you," she repeated, giving my hands a comforting squeeze.

"I don't know."

"He'll forgive you."

"But what if he doesn't? What would I do, Janice?"

"He'll forgive you," she insisted, her eyes clear and her gaze unwavering. Janice, the goofy girl with too much energy and oodles of heart, looked into my eyes and said exactly what I should have known she would say. "Just like I did."

I wish I could be as sure as she that James would forgive me. He had been hurt once by lies. Would this second time be too much for him?

Chapter Twenty-Two

"I did what you asked. I want my divorce." I stood rigidly in Joaquin's office. I squared my shoulders and tried to maintain my dignity. The marriage had all been a farce, no point in pretending he had any hurt feelings over it.

I had been a class-A fool for ever believing this man had fallen for me. If I had figured that out twelve years ago, I probably would have been a wreck. But now? I felt used. That weird moment up in the suite, when I'd thought for sure we'd end up having sex—I was sick to my stomach thinking about it.

Joaquin sat behind his desk, his fingers tented over the expensive mahogany. "I will sign the papers. You did a perfect job." His hazel eyes were nothing more than empty hollows to an empty soul. That man could feel nothing for any woman.

I wanted to tell him Mercedes knew our marriage had been a farce and that we were divorcing. But I didn't think it would hurt him as much as he had hurt the both of us. He would be angry, yes, but the hurt would not be the same.

Mercedes seemed to be over his lies. It probably wouldn't have helped her either.

I wasn't about to let him off so easily, though. He couldn't waltz back into my life, try to sleep with me, and end up ruining my relationship with James for nothing. His actions had to have some consequences. I tucked away that thought for later. Right now, I needed to get his signature on whatever papers the lawyer, Mr. Esposito, would have.

"I'll be back in touch this afternoon. If you're not here, I'll leave the papers with your secretary and pick them up tomorrow morning." I crossed my arms over my chest. "And then I never want to see you or hear from you again."

"Ah, *Querida*—"

"I told you not to call me that again," I seethed. "We both know there was never any love between us."

His mouth curled up into a sardonic smile. "Sometimes you don't need love," he said. He picked up a silver letter opener off of his desk and ran its flat blade against the palm of his hand. "You had something I wanted." His eyes locked onto mine and a jolt of sexual energy radiated from them. "And you let me take it. Simple as that." He turned the letter opener over in his hand, concentrating on its shining surface.

I shuddered at the coldness in those words.

"It's no longer yours for the taking, Joaquin. Tomorrow I'm leaving here and going back to a much better life than you'll ever have." I turned on my heel to leave, but not before I saw him clutch the sharp letter opener tightly in his hand, as if he were trying to squeeze the life out of it. I heard it clatter on the desk as I walked out the door and out of his life forever.

*

"So, you're going to stay?" Janice asked.

I dumped my shoes out of the ice bucket in my new suite and hung some of my clothes in the closet. "I don't know what I want to do to tell you the truth."

"I think you should stay."

"But what about James?"

"He's hurt. He's angry. You need to let him blow off some steam." She sat on the couch, watching me put my clothes away.

"I think I've lost him."

"You don't know that."

"But I feel it. The way he told me to leave—I'd never heard him sound like that before."

"He'll get over it."

"I don't think so."

"Oh, Suze." She got up from the couch and gave me a sympathetic hug, her bony body more bruising in an embrace than comforting.

"I think I just need to have my mind on something else."

"Even with Joaquin here?"

"I think I can manage. Now that I know the truth, he won't bother me anymore." I slipped my favorite sundress onto a hanger and stuck it in the closet. "All of that is over with. In the past."

"And you got him to sign the papers?"

I nodded. "The lawyer's sending them over today. It gets the process started. It takes six months for the whole thing to be over with, and it can't come soon enough."

She patted me on the back and walked over to the mini-fridge. "Well, so now that you're staying another three days, what do you want to do?" She stuck her head inside it. "Maybe try out the parasailing?"

"I don't think so."

Janice, unwrapping a Snickers bar she'd found, made a moue of disapproval.

"But," I said, "I think I'd be up for the intermediate kayaking class."

"You would?" she asked with a mouthful of chocolate and peanuts.

I nodded.

She swallowed and set the candy bar down on top of the fridge. "Just wait 'til I tell George! He won't believe it." She dashed to the phone by the bed. "Oh, and by the way, he's invited both of us on a river rafting trip."

She dialed the phone.

"Is that so?"

"I'm thinking next August? It'll be warm, but all the college kids will be back in school. What do you think?" She turned her attentions to George on the other end of the phone. "Oh, George! You'll never guess. Suzie said she'll take the class."

I continued to hang up my clothes while Janice chattered with George, making plans for the few remaining days of our trip. Dinner, excursions, kayaking—she was packing three vacations into one.

I owed it to her to stay. Be a friend. Do the things she had envisioned us doing together. Then, I could head home and tackle my relationship with James—if I had a relationship left to salvage.

*

The hot sun shined bright in my eyes, but I paddled for all I was worth. Our instructor, Enrique, proudly declared me certified to kayak on the open ocean yesterday, and I was determined to keep up with Janice, George, and his traveling buddies.

"Come on, Suzie! You can do it!" yelled Janice from her position, only fifteen yards in front of me.

I centered my concentration on the slick of the paddle against the waves. The burn in my upper arms told me my muscles worked hard to keep up with the quick pace of the rest of the group.

"Did you see it?" George cried out.

"A dolphin!" Janice crowed. "Oh my gosh! Right in between us. Did you see that, Suzie?"

My efforts were solely focused on moving my kayak forward, not on the sights around me. But I had caught up. I floated a mere yard away from Janice. "No, I missed it." I eased up on my paddling, letting the kayak cut through the salt water on its own momentum.

"Don't worry. I'm sure there'll be more."

George drifted alongside Janice now. We could talk without having to yell anymore.

"How much farther, do you think?" I looked across the bay to the point of land north of us. Janice's desire to kayak across the bay was coming true.

George squinted and looked up at the cliff's edge. "I'd say another couple miles at least."

I groaned.

"You can't tell me you aren't enjoying this. Can you believe the view from here?" Janice asked.

She was right. I *was* enjoying it. I didn't think I would, but each paddle, each drop of sweat, each mile crossed I felt more and more alive. Sailboats dotted the bay all around us, their colorful sails billowing in the strong sea breezes. Fisherman, motoring in with a pre-dawn catch, sped past us from time to time. There were even a few windsurfers this far out, jumping and sailing across the ragged waves.

Looking back at the shore, the bright green of the palm trees and the colorful hotel buildings made for a picturesque display. I couldn't believe I had paddled out so far all on my own.

"Hey, guys," called out one of George's friend—Jim or Tim or something like that, "I wanna get there before Christmas. Can we get a move on?"

I stuck my paddle in the water, pulling as hard as I could. My kayak cut through the waves, and joy filled my heart. A lightness of being that I'd never felt before. After the emotional turmoil of the last few days, it surprised me to feel renewed, alive, clean and unburdened for the first time in a long, long time.

"I'll race you," I yelled out to Janice, knowing I could never beat her. She was much stronger than I. But I didn't care. I wanted to paddle, to feel the wind in my hair and the sun on my face, and live.

"You're on," said my friend. The muscles stood out on her skinny arms, and she bore down on her paddle. "Let's see what you're made of, Eisenhart."

Chapter Twenty-Three

Our last morning in Acapulco I rolled my suitcase—more well-packed than when I arrived (the wheels actually rolled this time)—into the lobby. My key card had been handed in, and my flight for San Antonio was leaving in a couple of hours.

"So, you think you'll be okay going to the airport alone?" Janice asked. "I mean, my plane doesn't leave until tonight, but I don't mind hanging out with you for a few hours."

"Nah, don't worry about it. I'll be fine. Still got some of my book left to read." I held up a paperback book as proof. "And besides, I know you want to spend some time with George before you leave."

She blushed. "Oh, Suzie, he's such a great guy."

"I know."

"Who would have guessed I'd meet someone here of all places?"

"Why not?" I shrugged. "You're a great catch, babe."

She smiled at the compliment. "What do you think of him?"

"I think you know what I think of him already." We walked over to a bench near the entrance and sat down together. "He's perfect for you."

"You think so?"

"You know it's true. He follows you around like a little lost puppy."

She giggled at the description. "Do you think I'm nuts for thinking about moving to West Virginia?"

"No. I think it's about time you moved on. Did something just for you. Your firm has been sucking the life out of you for years."

"Yeah, but at least they paid well. I'll kinda miss that."

"No you won't."

She smiled. We both knew she'd be spending all her free time with George, which was a far cry from the way she'd been spending her free time in Chicago.

I gave her a hug. "You're probably the best friend a girl could have."

She waved a hand at me. "Oh, come on now."

"I'll never forget how important that is—ever." I looked her hard in the eye to let her know that I meant it.

"Stop it, or you're going to make me cry." She brushed her fingertips underneath her eye and sniffed.

"Promise me that we'll get together more often like this," I gestured at the tropical beauty right outside the glass doors. "I've missed you."

"I've missed you, too." We waited for my taxi to the airport to arrive.

"So," Janice said, "are you glad you took the sea kayaking course?"

I thought about our amazing paddle across the bay yesterday. "Definitely. But, personally, I was really disappointed to find the trapeze class had been cancelled indefinitely. I mean, why come to Acapulco if you can't brush up on your acrobatic skills?" I gave her a grin.

She jabbed me with her elbow. "All right. Maybe that's not your thing—but George and me, maybe next time we're here, we could try it out."

George and Janice were the perfect pair—I had never seen two people eat so much and work out so hard. Sickening. They would probably have dozens of dark-haired, long-limbed children who could out-run, out-bike, out-swim, and out-raft the whole state of West Virginia.

I relished a last chat with Janice before I headed home. After twelve years, my mind finally cleared of worry. I felt freer than I had in a long, long time.

Sitting in the lobby and waiting with Janice, I patted my purse and the copy of the important papers I stowed there. The official copy of our divorce papers would be filed by my attorney. I had left a packet for *Señor* Esposito at the reception desk, who would be picking it up later today.

But the copy I carried was just for me. Something to remind me of my mistakes and remind me of the important things in my life. Not what my mother or my best friend thought of me, but being honest about who I was.

I wanted to shout in that bustling lobby: *Here I am, Suzette Eisenhart, and I am divorced.*

"Hey, I think your taxi's here." Janice pointed out the glass lobby doors at the yellow-and-black Volkswagen Bug waiting in the circular drive.

Coolest taxi ever.

God, I loved this country.

"Well, guess this is it," I announced.

"Yep. Have a safe flight."

"Thanks, sweetie." I gave her one last hug, and then grabbed the handle of my suitcase. Nothing remained here for me. I'd finished what I'd set out to do. Now, I needed to get back to the San Antonio and see if I could salvage my relationship with James.

I climbed in the back seat of the Bug while the driver stuffed my suitcase into the front storage trunk. Janice stood inside the doors of the hotel, waving and smiling.

I waved back as the cab pulled away from the curb.

I thought about James and our little green-and-white

house in the suburbs. It had all been so perfect. Too perfect to last maybe. Several times on the drive to the airport, I wished I could have called him. But even if I could, who knew if he would answer.

I wasn't sure if he would be waiting for me when I got back home, but I would accept whatever decision he made. All was not lost. I loved him, and I thought he could love me again. It might take him some time, but I hoped he would forgive me.

I thought of his angular face that was more interesting than handsome and the way his lanky body moved on the tennis court, gangling and awkward. Yet he could still serve the best smash I'd ever seen.

He might not be waiting for me at the airport when I got back, but he would be there. Somewhere in San Antonio. I would find him. I would make things work again.

"*Señorita?*" The taxi driver pulled into the airport, the engine of his car rumbling and spewing black exhaust into the air.

"Oh, we're here."

"*Sí. Puede usted que le ayudo?*" My driver gestured at the heavy, bolder-like suitcase sitting on the curb.

"No," I shook my head at him. "I don't need any help. I can manage all by myself."

I exited the cab into the bright, hot sunshine of Acapulco, and, for the first time the heat didn't stifle me.

Chapter Twenty-Four

April 2005 - Seven Months Later

"Tall, non-fat latte with a shot of hazelnut," I told the barista behind the counter at my favorite coffeehouse a few miles from home. My life might be dramatically different than before that trip to Acapulco, but my drink preferences had stayed the same.

The woman at the register took the ten dollar bill out of my hand and swapped it for some change.

I picked out a seat by the big plate glass window in front and waited for my order. The weather, which had been hot the day I left for Acapulco, was cool and rainy. That pouring down, lightning-and-thunder kind of rain that sweeps across Texas, pounds out the dust, and then disappears as fast as it arrives.

It was Saturday. The house I'd once shared with James felt too large, too empty, and too dark today. I wanted to be out with people, noise, and activity. My seat by the window did an adequate job of distracting me.

The home improvement store next to the coffeehouse attracted a constant stream of shoppers. People loaded lumber, PVC pipe, and grass seed into trucks, minivans, and even an old, beat-up station wagon.

"Tall, non-fat latte with a shot of hazelnut!" A teenage boy called out from behind the counter.

I hopped off the high stool and went to collect my drink.

As I sipped my latte, I wondered where James would be on a rainy Saturday afternoon. The image of his face, half-smiling, his dimple in full force, popped into my brain. Regret tugged in my gut, but I pushed back any bad feelings about the way things ended.

When I arrived back in San Antonio no one had been there to greet me. No car had waited near Baggage Claim to pick me up.

On the plane, I couldn't resist picking up the air phone and dialing James's cell. I wanted to listen to his voicemail message, but that warm honey of a voice made me want to say something. I'm sorry. Forgive me. I love you.

I'd almost said it, too.

But then, I realized I needed to back off. Making rash decisions and rash comments had gotten me into trouble in the first place. A man like James deserved some distance, some time—to bombard him with my feelings and my apologies now would do nothing.

So I arrived in San Antonio with my luggage and a divorce.

When the taxi dropped me off at our little green-and-white house, I knew James would be gone. Even from the outside, although nothing really had changed—the flowerbeds were overrun with crab grass and the backyard fence was missing one of its slats—I knew something was different.

Walking through the front door, I saw the coat rack. His trench coat was gone, and it was sunny and ninety-five degrees outside. Then I knew for sure that he'd left, and he wasn't going to come back.

At first, I didn't want to look any further. I dropped my suitcase on the entryway floor, set my handbag on the sofa table, and sat down, staring at the sage green walls of our living room. Maybe if I didn't look any further, I would be mistaken. Maybe he was still at work. Maybe he would be back soon, folding laundry or watching the basketball game on TV.

So I sat there on the couch for hours, watching the sun make its way across the floor in hot white patches of light.

That had been months ago.

Even though we worked for the same company, we never saw each other. He worked in development, and I worked as a technical writer. We focused on different products. I kept my nose to the grindstone and buried myself in bulleting target ideas, formatting tables and charts, and indexing technical terminology.

And I kept that very important paper in my desk. I waited for the weeks to pass, for the divorce to become final. I wouldn't feel completely unburdened from my past until that day. Six months of waiting to be single again—for real.

I made a new weekend routine to replace the Saturday morning breakfast-in-bed I'd shared with James for almost four years. Saturdays were my new 'special' day. I got up early, washed a couple loads of laundry, and then made my way to one of several coffee places within a short drive of the house.

This morning I'd chosen The Coffee Beanery. Horrible name (I mean, what's a 'beanery'?) but fantastic coffee and a great people-watching window. Those were the key elements for me. I read the paper, sipped my coffee, and watched the Saturday morning crowds ebb and flow in the parking lot.

I sat for several hours watching the daily lives of San Antonians play out before me. Once I got jacked up on caffeine or my butt got too sore from sitting on the padded stool, I'd go home.

This morning, five sips away from my caffeine max for the day, I saw the car.

His car.

James's car.

If my heart wasn't already beating a million miles a minute from the two lattes I'd consumed, I'm sure it would have beaten as fast because of that car. A 1998 maroon Volkswagen Jetta with a small dent in the front fender from the time I tried to parallel park by the Riverwalk. Not my finest moment.

His car has been parked twenty-five yards out, in the sea of other cars. The rain had slowed to a drizzling grayness, making it easier to distinguish it from all the rest.

My ex-fiancé climbed out of it, his long, thin limbs unfolding like a Swiss Army Knife.

I fiddled nervously with the handle on my coffee cup. I wanted to walk up to him, ask him to forgive me, and have everything go back to the way it was. But life is never that simple.

James wove between parked cars, making his way toward the sporting goods store. His familiar, awkward gait vanished from view, and that's when I made my move.

I got up from the stool and self-bussed my mug in the white bin by the garbage can. For a moment I wished I wore something a little less slob-on-a-Saturday morning: gray yoga pants, a faded yellow hoodie with a hole on the elbow, and the I-haven't-washed-my-hair-since-yesterday-morning ponytail.

I reminded myself he had seen me under much worse circumstances. Strengthening my resolve, I left the coffee house and pulled the yellow hood up over my head to keep off the drizzle.

*

I waited by his car, watching for him. I was soaked through. Thank goodness the rain had stopped after only a few minutes of standing in it. The weak sun peeked out from behind patches of clouds. A nice Saturday was on its way after all.

James emerged from the sporting goods store, a large bag in one hand. He looked up, and his gaze locked onto me. He paused in his steps for a moment, but he kept heading straight for me.

A shiver ran through me.

When he came within a few feet of me, I said, "Looks like you could use some help."

Wordlessly, he looked from me to his right front tire, which was as flat as a pancake.

"Suzie, what are you doing here?"

"I'm here to help you. Can you pop the trunk and get out the spare?"

He set the bag down next to me, and pressed a button on his keychain. "When did you learn how to change a tire?"

I could hear the beginning of a smile in his voice, but I didn't look up. We had a tenuous connection I didn't want to break.

He handed me the jack, and I got down on my knees to set it under the frame of the car.

"Oh, somebody I once knew taught me how—" My mind flashed back to the night I met James—his hands on mine, showing me how to use the jack and how to loosen the lug nuts. Everything about him that night had been determined, masculine, and precise.

"Oh, really?"

I looked up and caught his green-eyed gaze. I missed their warmth and their softness. No other man had eyes like those.

The words tumbled out of my mouth, "I'm sorry, James. So, so sorry." Before he could react, I bent my head down, ratcheting the handle to lift the car up higher. "I was nineteen, and I was an idiot. I didn't know what to do. I never wanted to hurt you. Never."

His hand touched my hair—a cool, soft touch. "Oh, Suze," he said with a voice full of misery and hurt. "You could have told me."

"I know," I whispered.

He was right. I could have. If I knew this man so well, I should have known he would understand, but I never even gave him the chance.

My cold, wet fingers slipped on the lug nuts. I tried to use the damp sleeve of my raggedy hoodie to get a better grasp.

He stood there for a moment, his hand on my head. The weight of it comforted me. Then, he walked to the trunk to wrestle out the spare.

I took a deep breath, my heart pounding furiously, and asked, "Why don't I buy you a cup of coffee?"

James set the spare down next to me. I kept cranking the jack. "What about pie? There has to be pie."

My heart beat faster. "Coconut cream?"

"Hell yes."

I laughed. Lightness and air filling me from head to toe. He became my James again, my sweet, silly James.

When we finished changing the tire, we headed back to The Coffee Beanery. We walked side-by-side. I wanted to grasp his hand in mine, but knew that something like this needed lots of time, lots of care.

As we strolled closer to the coffeehouse, I slipped the cap to the tire's air valve into my pocket. I hoped James wouldn't notice it was missing, but if he did, I think he would forgive me.

He held the door open for me, and I walked inside, but not before I caught his gaze and saw that green softness. Something I thought I wouldn't ever see again.

In one hand he carried the large bag from the sporting goods store. I wondered why he didn't put it in his trunk, but when we sat down to drink our coffee in a quiet corner, he showed me why.

He set the bag on the table and pulled out my tennis racket.

I thought I'd misplaced it all these months. I gave him a quizzical look.

"Your racket's needed to be restrung for a long time. I finally got around to getting it done." He handed me the familiar worn grip of my Prince racket. I accepted it and laid it on the table, staring at him in surprise.

"I forgive you, Suze."
That was all I needed to hear.

Epilogue

I tucked a copy of my finalized divorce papers into an envelope, addressed the front, and placed enough stamps on it for postage to Mexico.

I glanced at the name on the front, "Mercedes Ruiz," and hoped that her parents would get it to her. Wherever she was.

I thought of the picture of Ariana in Joaquin's office—the smiling, pretty girl with eyes so much like her father's. She deserved better.

But maybe this will help, I thought, carrying the letter out to the mailbox. For on those finalized divorce papers was Joaquin's new address in Cancún. *He thought he had been so clever, trying to get away from Ariana and his responsibilities*, I thought to myself, as I lifted the red flag on the side of the mailbox.

"Time for dinner!" called out James, his head peeking out from our front door.

"I'm coming," I called out, giving one last glance at the mailbox. Then, smiling to myself, I followed James into our house and shut the door behind me.

ACAPULCO NIGHTS

About the Author

K. J. Gillenwater survived life as a military linguist and a technical writer before pursuing her dreams to become the novelist she'd wanted to be since grade school. She writes what she loves: suspense and romance. When she isn't writing, K. J. loves to watch way too much T.V., bake, hang out with her family and enjoy the view from her front porch.

If you enjoyed this book, K. J. Gillenwater is the author of three paranormal suspense books, which are available in print and in eBook format through Amazon and Barnes & Noble.

The Ninth Curse

His blood for a cure. It's a cruel and deadly bargain...

Nine curses. Nine weeks to live. Joel Hatcher has inherited more than a family legacy. It's a time bomb that's ticking down to the inevitable: his own death. But the curse won't die with him. Unless he can find a way to break the cycle, his younger brother becomes the next victim.

In the throes of the third curse, the Painful Pox, Joel makes a last-ditch decision to seek the help of a young spiritualist.

One look into Joel's suffering eyes, and "Madame Eugenie" finds herself torn between doing the right thing and fulfilling her most secret wish—bring her husband Adam back from the dead. Joel's cursed blood is the missing ingredient in her resurrection rituals, and Adam's spirit whispers seductively that there's only one way to get it: steal it.

As Gen and Joel unearth his family's past to track down a cure, they come closer to each other, and to a horrible truth. To live, Joel must lose everything. Including the woman he has grown to love.

Warning: This book contains curses, sacrifices, a ghostly husband, a crazy cat and a love that defies all odds.

The Little Black Box

After the suspicious suicides of several student test subjects, Paula Crenshaw, research assistant and budding telekinetic in Paranormal Sciences at Blackridge University, suspects they may be connected to a little black box designed to read auras. Professor Jonas Pritchard, the head of the department, doesn't believe his precious experiment could be causing students to drop like flies.

But when her best friend almost dies after her encounter with the black box, Paula is certain there is a connection. She pulls her cute, but sloppy, office buddy, Will Littlejohn, into the mystery, and they get closer to the truth behind who might be financially backing the project and why. Haunted by memories of a childhood accident, which she believes she caused with her untamed psychic abilities, Paula finds herself lured to the black box and its mysteries.

Blood Moon

Werewolves are roaming Northeast High, and Savannah Black is determined to hunt them down.

When Savannah's academic rival mysteriously disappears, she enlists the aid of her two best friends, Dina and Nick, to solve the mystery. Football players with glowing eyes and razor sharp canine teeth may have fooled the faculty, but not Savannah and her friends.

These brave students are determined to eradicate a clan of deadly werewolves who threaten to take over their school. When Dina disappears right before the big Homecoming Dance, Savannah and Nick must act quickly to save her from the werewolf's curse. But will a straight-A student be able to master knives and silver bullets as easily as chemistry and calculus?

Warning! This book contains pentagrams, bonfires, and 1000 SAT words and their definitions to challenge you.

Printed in Great Britain
by Amazon